THE RANCHER

LILY GRAISON

The Rancher
The Willow Creek Series Book #4

ISBN: 9781799006985

Cover design by Clarise Tan
http://www.ctcovercreations.com

Visit Lily's website at www.lilygraison.com

THE RANCHER

PROLOGUE

Missoula, Montana Territory

As visions went, she was by far the most alluring one he'd seen in years.

Holden turned up his glass, swallowed what remained inside, and kept his gaze locked on the woman making her way to the bar. The hem of her brown sateen skirt swept the sawdust floor, the light from the lanterns catching in the shiny material of her dress and drawing his eye to places no decent man should look, but the soft curve of her breasts was too tempting to glance away from.

He'd seen many beautiful women in his thirty-two years but something about this woman left him dazed. It was probably the amount of whiskey he'd drank, or the fact the light was so dim inside the saloon, but she looked ethereal, like some other-world being straight from one of those fairytale books his daughter Alex had stacked in her room.

His gaze swept over her again. Her dark hair was left loose, long curls bouncing free over her shoulders and when she put

1

her back to him, he traced the line of her spine to her narrow waist, the gentle flair of her hips to her rounded behind and he felt his throat go dry despite the amount of alcohol he'd consumed.

He sat up straight in his seat and tore his gaze from her to sweep over the room again.

His brother, Tristan, had told him this was the best gaming house in all of Missoula and from what he'd seen, Tristan had been right. It was clean, the whiskey was good and the whores were pretty and smelled like a woman should, but picking one to spend the evening with wasn't easy. The blondes reminded him of his late wife, God rest her soul, and the brunettes weren't as buxom as he liked. Of course, they all paled in comparison to the beauty who caught the attention of those not too drunk to notice.

He turned his gaze back to the bar. She was still there, her face reflected in the mirror on the wall. She wasn't a whore, that much he knew. She was too refined looking, not to mention she'd entered from the street and was now ordering a drink from the looks of it. A lady who drank in public. That was new.

Picking up his empty glass, he stood, waded through the crowd and approached the bar with one goal in mind. He had to get a closer look at this woman to see if it was the alcohol making her so breathtaking.

He stopped beside her, ordered another drink, and glanced up at her in the mirror, then turned to where she stood. She was staring down into her glass, the amber liquid untouched. "As whiskey goes, it's not bad," he said.

She turned her head to him and he'd be damned if his heart didn't give a little kick in his chest. Her eyes were the oddest shade of brown he'd ever seen. They reminded him of the whiskey in her glass, a light, swirling amber. The rest of her face was remarkable too. Her complexion was smooth, her lips plump and pink. Small curls framed her face making her look soft and feminine. Beautiful.

He blinked and nodded to her glass. "Do you always order whiskey then just stare at it?"

She tilted her head a little to one side. "Why are you talking to me?"

Holden opened his mouth to answer but closed it with a snap. Beautiful and rude. He smiled and leaned one arm on the bar. "To be honest, now that you ask, I've no idea."

She stared at him for long moments before smiling and looking back at her glass. "Honesty. That's a rare attribute for a man."

He raised an eyebrow. "Depends on the man, I suppose."

Her head turned, those whiskey colored eyes giving him a look from head to toe. "Really? I didn't think any man was capable of it."

Holden laughed. "Beautiful, rude and bitter. A strange combination."

Amusement filled her eyes and she turned her body to face him. "I'm also surly, mean-spirited and suspicious."

"And you apparently don't care what others think."

"What makes you say that?"

Holden thumbed up the front of his hat. "I don't know of any lady who would walk into a saloon and order a whiskey at the bar, then stick around to drink it." He glanced down at her glass. "Or stare at it."

She shrugged one delicate shoulder. "Who says I'm a lady?" She lifted her glass, slung back her whiskey as if she'd been doing it for years and grinned at him while setting the glass back down.

Holden swallowed his own liquor, nodded to the bartender to refill their glasses and never took his eyes off of her. "I'm Hol…"

"Don't!"

Holden shut his mouth, one eyebrow raised as she yelled at him, her right arm raised as if to ward off the words. Her cheeks pinkened before she straightened her spine.

"No names, please."

He grinned. "Okay."

She sighed, her shoulders relaxing. "I find it much easier to just talk to someone without really knowing who they are."

"Mysterious, rude, bitter and beautiful. Now I'm intrigued."

She flashed him a tiny smile. "Stop trying to flatter me."

"Who says I am?"

She laughed, the sound a tinkling vibration that coursed through his body and ended near his toes. Her eyes sparkled as she laughed, and he knew before the night was out he'd be so smitten with this woman he'd never get her out of his head.

They talked for close to an hour about nothing specific, consumed more whiskey than he'd drunk in months, and when the crowd inside the saloon grew rowdy, their voices raised to the point he couldn't hear what she was saying, she raised up on her toes, her mouth next to his ear, and asked if he'd like to take a walk with her. All thought of buying companionship for the evening was forgotten.

Out on the wooden sidewalk, she turned and stumbled, her laughter like music as he reached out his arm to steady her. "I think you may have had too much to drink."

"Are you saying I'm drunk?" She leaned against him and grinned, taking hold of his arm and looping hers through his before turning them and starting down the sidewalk.

Holden inhaled a breath, her rose scented skin infusing the air around him. "I'd never insult a lady in such a way."

She laughed again, proving she had more to drink than she was used to and looked up at him with those alluring eyes. "I'm far from drunk, sir, I can assure you. I would have never left the saloon with you had I been."

He smiled. "So you would have passed out on the floor instead?"

"Probably." She inhaled a deep breath, raising her head. "Do you live here?"

"I thought you didn't want to know anything about me?"

She gave him a sideways look. "I don't. The less I know about you the better off I'll be, but it's so warm for fall. I'm just trying to find out if it's always this way in Montana."

It took an effort to mask his disappointment in her not wanting to know who he really was but he shrugged it off. "No. It'll start cooling down soon and once winter sets in, you'll wish you were somewhere else."

"I doubt that."

She stopped in front of one of the many hotels in town and turned to face him. Her eyes were drowsy looking, her lips glistening with moisture from where she'd licked them and he'd never wanted to kiss anyone the way he did her. "Is this where you're staying?"

"Yes."

He should have picked this hotel, too. He'd chosen the more expensive one down the road and almost wished he could check in here and go grab his things so he could spend his last evening in town with her close by.

The past week had been hard, a physical and mental drain on his body. Selling off his horses, paying the wranglers and then watching them as they all grabbed a woman in the saloon and headed upstairs planted a seed of longing in him that he hadn't felt in ages. Being so far from home, he could indulge in any manner of debauchery and once the idea was there, he couldn't seem to let it go.

Alex, his ten-year-old daughter, was too impressionable to go traipsing off to town to find his comfort with one of the whores at the Diamond Back Saloon in Willow Creek and the dull ache from years of denying his body the pleasure of a woman was felt in every muscle and every nerve. He'd spent an extra night in town just to see those aches eased. No one at home would know, least of all Alex, and the moment he decided to pick one of those pretty ladies at the saloon, in walks a woman who put the others to shame.

She was still looking up at him, her whiskey colored eyes sparkling in the moonlight and his entire body jolted while looking at her. He wanted her. Wanted her unlike anything he'd wanted in a long time but saying so would ruin the entire evening.

They stood staring at one another for long minutes, the crowd on the street and sidewalks disappearing and when she smiled at him, the look in her eyes telling him she was thinking the same thing he was, his heart started racing.

"If I wasn't a lady, I'd be tempted to ask you up to my room."

Holden's fingers clenched into fists at his side. "If you weren't a lady, I'd take you up on it."

She licked her lips and Holden's gaze was drawn to her mouth while every nerve in his body jumped, screamed, and demanded he forget his manners. To take advantage of the situation, damn his conscience and take her to bed. Spend the rest of the night between her thighs and make his way home come morning with a memory he'd have a hard time forgetting.

The wind blew a strand of her hair into her eyes and he pushed it away, tucking it behind her ear. The moment he touched her, caught the faintest scent of roses on her skin, his heart pounded so hard, he had trouble breathing around it.

She stared up at him, an invitation in her eyes. "I'm in room twelve. Give me ten minutes."

Turning, she left him standing on the sidewalk and entered the hotel, glancing back over her shoulder to smile at him. He had one night in Missoula and even though he'd never see this woman again, he'd carry the memory of her with him always. The way she'd looked at him said she would too. The invitation to her room was there and he wasn't stupid enough to pass on it.

CHAPTER 1

GOOD LORD ABOVE, the man was all but naked!

Laurel blinked and nearly ran the wagon into the fence as she stared at him. She managed to stop the horses and even remembered to set the brake on the wagon, reminding herself that she was a lady and averted her gaze.

Alexandra Avery fidgeted in the seat beside her and Laurel gave her a nod of her head, watching as the girl stood and jumped from the wagon, running to whom she assumed was her father. The man leaned down as the girl rushed out an explanation and when he turned his head to look her way, and she got a good look at his face, Laurel's heart skipped a beat as it slammed against her ribcage. "Oh, sweet heavens, no." It couldn't be!

He stood to his full height, his eyes widening a fraction as he looked at her, before he grinned so devilishly, her breath caught. She knew in an instant she was in trouble.

How in the world did she end up in the same town as him? The odds were too fantastic to even imagine.

Memories of them together screamed through her head as she stared at him. She'd spent every day since that night in Missoula trying to forget about him. So far, she'd managed to only think of him once or twice a day but seeing him again, standing right in front of her with nothing but his trousers, hat, and a smile on, she cursed her luck.

Squaring her shoulders, Laurel climbed from the borrowed wagon and tried to keep her focus on his face as she crossed the space to where he stood. It wasn't easy. Not with the way the sun glinted off the sweat on his chest, the small beads of perspiration shimmering like small jewels and drawing her gaze to the hard lines of his naked torso. She'd felt those muscles against her hands, kissed them with lips that still tingled just thinking about it and she was near dizzy by the time she reached him.

She lifted her chin, determined to keep her gaze on his face, and hoped he couldn't hear her stammering heart beat. "Mr. Avery?" His gaze bore into her and Laurel's heart screeched to a stop before it pounded so hard she fought for breath. She cleared her throat and blinked, trying to regain her composure.

When she knew her voice wouldn't squeak, she said, "I'm Laurel Montgomery, the new school teacher."

The grin on his face grew as if he knew some wicked secret he wasn't about to share with her. But Laurel knew his secrets. Well, the ones he'd displayed for her one warm fall night in Missoula four weeks ago.

Laurel glanced at Alexandra, his daughter, apparently, her little arms crossed over her chest and an identical smirk was on her face. She stared at her, trying to come to grips with the fact she'd more than likely slept with a married man. The guilt that followed caused the butterflies swimming in her stomach to die and her stomach ached to the point she felt ill.

She lifted her head, cleared her throat and met his smiling eyes with bitter resentment growing in her heart. "I've been meaning to meet all the parents of my students and you were first on my list."

"I'm flattered." The look in his eyes changed and Laurel knew he was remembering that night too. Damn his hide. Why did he have to live here?

His voice was just as deep as she remembered and the sound of it caressed her flesh as if he'd physically touched her. Goose bumps prickled her arms and she ignored the feeling, trying to remember all she planned to say to him. "Don't be flattered, Mr. Avery. What I have to tell you is far from becoming." Laurel turned her gaze on Alexandra, throwing her a disapproving look before facing him again. "I'm sorry to say your daughter is a menace and has disrupted my class on a daily basis."

That got his attention. The smile vanished and when he looked down at Alexandra, the girl's puffed-up pose, deflated. "What did you do?"

Alexandra huffed out a breath, her hands curled into fists. "Jesse started it. He said I was the ugliest boy he'd ever seen so, I popped him one." She grinned. "He cried like a little girl."

Laurel exhaled, exasperated. "He most certainly did not, Alexandra. You're telling stories again."

The girl whirled on her, her arm flung to point at her. "And she won't stop calling me Alexandra. I've told her a hundred times, pa, my name is Alex, but she just won't say it."

Laying his hand on Alexandra's shoulder, the girl quieted instantly. When he looked up, amusement shined in his eyes. "She doesn't like to be called Alexandra."

"I've noticed but that isn't reason enough to disrupt my classroom everyday without fail."

"No, it's not."

Laurel glanced at Alexandra before straightening her spine and looking back up. "Can we speak alone, please?"

Something in his eyes said she'd made a mistake in making that small request. The smile that followed said as much too. He told Alex to wait on the front porch for him and when he turned to face her again, Laurel felt instantly exposed. His gaze never left her face but she knew he was picturing her naked. It was in the smile he gave her, the way his eyelids lowered just a fraction, as if he too was remembering that night. A night, she knew now, spelled trouble. Trouble she didn't want or need, regardless of the fact he was the most tempting thing she'd ever clapped eyes on.

She swallowed the sudden lump forming in her throat and pulled at the high collar of her dress. The sun was unbearably hot today for early fall. Much too hot.

Turning her head to avoid looking at him, she watched Alexandra run to the house, her boy trousers and chambray shirt causing a sigh to escape her. "She looks nothing like a girl."

"No, and she prefers it that way."

Realizing she'd spoken out loud, Laurel's face heated. "I meant no offense. It's just... well, I've never seen a girl act so boyish in all my life."

He laughed and leaned against the fence rail, the whiteness of those boards making the tanned hue of his skin even darker. His arm, propped on the top rail, was well muscled and Laurel's stomach clenched tight at the sight of it. She'd held on to those arms, felt them around her body and a tremor rushed through her limbs at the remembrance.

Laurel blinked and tried to remember why she'd made the trip out to his home. She had to clear her throat and swallow twice just to moisten her mouth enough to speak. "She's started three fights this week." Her voice cracked but she found it easier to talk keeping her focus on his chin instead of his eyes. "She also spits, has nothing to do with the other girls in class and her attire is inappropriate for her gender." She paused, bitterness closing her throat as her next words ate at her conscience. "I can't believe your wife would allow her daughter to grow up to be so... boyish."

He smiled again. "You're going to act as if we don't know each other, aren't you?"

Her heart skipped another beat. "I think, under the circumstances, that would be wise."

"Why?"

She laughed and looked up to meet his gaze. "Because I'm the new school teacher here, that's why. I have a certain reputation to uphold and if the town council knew…"

"That you frequented saloons and invited strange men into your bed, they'd put you on the first stagecoach out of town?"

Her face blazed hot. "Don't you dare judge me."

"I'm not." His gaze lowered to her breasts for a second before lifting again. "I just don't expect you to treat me as if we're strangers."

"As far as the people who live in this town are concerned, Mr. Avery, we are strangers."

He laughed that wonderful laugh again and Laurel had to look away. She gazed into the pasture, noticed a few horses grazing beyond the fence and tried to will her pulse to calm. Why did this have to happen? Why now?

"I've been thinking about you."

"Don't." She looked back at him and for the first time since meeting him, wished she never had. "I don't want to be reminded of it."

He lifted an eyebrow at her. "I was under the impression you enjoyed it as much as I did."

She bit her tongue to keep from blurting out she had. That she couldn't stop thinking about him, too, and as much as she'd enjoyed their one night together, it was a mistake. She glanced back at the house, saw Alexandra on the porch steps and tried to steer the conversation back to the girl. "Where is your wife?"

"She died after giving birth to Alex."

Remorse washed through her system, a knot of sorrow filling her stomach. "I'm sorry."

He nodded his head at her. "It was a long time ago." He sighed and lifted his hat, running his fingers through his hair before resettling it again. "We've not had a woman's influence at home until two years ago and honestly, I don't know a thing about girls." His gaze lowered from her face, sweeping down across her breasts and lower. "Well, I know nothing about little girls."

Her face heated again. The sun was indeed unbearable. Laurel pulled at her high collar and tried to convince herself it wasn't him causing her blood to heat and her skin to blaze as if she was cooking under the Montana sun.

A simple glance at his face caused her thoughts to run rampant. How she ended up in the town he lived in the most prevalent. She knew nothing about him other than he had a daughter and his wife had passed. Before today, she hadn't even known that much and she preferred it that way. Seeing him now though, his skin glistening with moisture, her fingers itched to touch him one last time. Her lips tingled with remembrance of his kisses and a tiny voice in the back of her head whispered she could have it all again.

She blinked, tried to quiet her body's demands and remembered why she was here. "Be that as it may, your daughter is a hellion. I'd think a man would want his daughter to be taught manners. She'll not catch a husband acting the way she does."

He laughed. "She's ten. I think I have a while until I have to worry about marrying her off."

"Maybe so, but if you continue to let her behave the way she does, you'll have a young lady who prefers to spit, curse and wear men's trousers. How hard do you think it will be to get her to change her ways then?"

The look on his face turned thoughtful, small lines bracketing his mouth. When he turned to look at the house, Laurel breathed a sigh of relief. It was much easier to talk to him when she didn't have to look at him. "Baby steps is what I suggest. One small change followed by another until she at least resembles a girl in looks and nature."

He turned back to face her, the lines still framing his wonderful mouth, and Laurel focused on his eyes so she wouldn't become distracted.

"I'll have a talk with her. She'll not cause you anymore trouble."

"I hope you're right." Laurel knew their conversation about Alexandra was over but stood like a deaf mute while staring at him. Something about this man was just too mesmerizing. His eyes were so perfectly blue, his teeth white and straight. The hard lines of muscle bisecting his abdomen, the definition of his chest…

She blinked and took a deep breath. "Well then, I'll just be on my way." She forced herself to turn and all but ran back to the wagon. Lifting her skirts to climb up, he grabbed her arm and she shrieked, jumped back and could only stare as he stood there grinning at her.

"This conversation isn't over."

"It is." Laurel inhaled several deep breaths, willing her heart to stop pounding. "I didn't want to know anything about you for a reason. I didn't want any attachments, then, now or ever. What we had is all there will ever be so there's no use discussing it. Now, if you'll excuse me, Mr. Avery, I have three more families to visit this evening."

He offered her his hand again. Common sense told her to ignore him but something inside of her caused butterflies to dance in erratic patterns every time she looked at him. That part of her screamed to accept. To touch him one last time. She lifted her hand and placed it in his while that same voice screamed what a fool she was.

The smile he gave her when his fingers closed around her hand all but took her breath. It hitched in her throat when he lifted her hand, placed a small kiss on her palm, desire shining bright in his eyes. "Since you refused to hear it in Missoula, my name is Holden and I'll definitely be seeing you again, Laurel."

She ignored him best she could, climbed into the wagon seat with his help and settled her skirts, grabbed the reins in hands much too sweaty for a proper lady to admit and flicked a glance back at him. "Seeing as you live here and avoiding you will be impossible, I would appreciate it if you would keep our future meetings on a professional level. I'm your daughter's teacher. Nothing more."

"That's not going to happen," he said. "I cursed myself for a fool the morning I left Missoula and was halfway home before I turned around and went back. You'd already checked out of the hotel." He tipped his hat to her, took two steps back and gave her a look that sent tingles racing down her spine. "I'll remind you every chance I get of what we shared, Laurel, and you can count on that."

Laurel clenched her teeth and flicked the reins, willed the horses to run, and was headed back to the road before her heart stopped racing. She was tempted to look over her shoulder but refused to do so.

Spending the night in Missoula instead of traveling on was a mistake. She knew that now but at the time, she'd wanted one last night. One night to just be herself. To walk into the saloon and not care what people thought. To order a drink, let all her troubles wash away with strong whiskey and not have a care in the world come morning.

That hadn't happened though. Not exactly. She'd met him, Holden Avery, moments after walking inside the saloon and that little voice in the back of her mind had whispered seductively to her that it was her last chance. The last chance to throw her inhibitions to the wind and just grab onto life one more time. And she had. She'd invited Holden to her room and spent hours having the most life altering sex of her life. She'd never had a man so attentive in her bed. Her body had burned, her lungs ached with need of air as he took her to heights she never knew existed again and again until she lay exhausted in his arms, his fingers and lips playing over her skin until she'd fallen asleep.

Her body still tingled in remembrance of his touch and that little voice in her head was whispering she could have it again.

That her desire for him could be sated night after night. She refused to listen. She couldn't get involved with him. Ever. Regardless of how much she wanted to.

She rode under the curved arch leaving Avery Ranch and she couldn't stop from turning her head, peering over her shoulder to where she'd left Holden standing.

He was still watching her.

LAUREL WAS clean out of sight before Holden turned toward the house. He could see Alex sitting on the steps, her elbows propped on her knees and knew, regardless of what he said, she would fight him until she was blue in the face.

He walked back to the fence, grabbed his shirt and slipped it on, smiling to himself as he buttoned it. After four weeks of wondering, in one afternoon he'd not only found the temptress he couldn't seem to forget but he also learned her name was Laurel and where she lived. Right here in Willow Creek of all places. His heart gave a powerful thump with the newfound knowledge.

Many a night he'd lain awake thinking of her. Wondering if he'd ever see her again. Wishing he'd done things a bit different all those weeks ago. He would have taken his time, for one, forgoing sleep entirely to spend one more hour looking at her. Touching her. Tasting her kisses and savoring those little noises she made as they lay skin to skin. He hadn't even minded she didn't want to know his name and refused to tell him hers. At the time, he'd been without a woman for so long, he hadn't cared. Not until later, when he was halfway home and couldn't stop thinking about her. It's why he'd turned around and went back. He hadn't wanted to let her go. He'd wanted her to the point his body ached with it. A shiver raced up his spine again as he remembered their night together.

He started for the house, his gaze locked on Alex and wondered what she'd done at school. He knew she was rowdy but he'd never had any of her previous teachers tell him she was unruly and the fact Laurel did, left him feeling uncomfortable.

He hadn't told her he had a daughter, she hadn't wanted to know anything about him, and now that she knew, he wondered what she thought about it.

His mind drifted further and further toward Laurel as he approached the house and he mentally berated himself for not taking the time to meet the town's new teacher when she arrived. Four wasted weeks had gone by with Laurel in town and by the time he made it into the yard he knew, half the men in the surrounding area had probably seen Laurel. He'd have to fight them off with a stick to keep them from trying to court her.

She was the finest looking woman he'd seen in ages and with women being a scarce thing in this area, she'd have suitors lined up the length of town asking for her hand in marriage. The whole idea left a bad taste in his mouth. He couldn't imagine her with someone else. He wouldn't. As far as he was concerned, Laurel Montgomery was his. He'd make her want him like he wanted her, even if he had to tame his hellion of a daughter to do so.

Alex glared at him when he stopped at the steps. The frown on her face said it all. She wasn't going to be cowed by him or anyone. He sighed and readjusted his hat. "Have you been giving the new school teacher a hard time?"

She rolled her eyes. "She's too uppity, pa. Makes us say please and thank you for everything."

"That's just good manners, Alex, not being uppity."

"Same difference." She stood up, stared him in the eye, and braced her hands on her hips. "She said we can't spit, we can't say anything mean to anyone or tease them and we have to act like perfect ladies and gentlemen at all times."

"There's nothing wrong with that."

Her eyes widened. "I'm ten. Why I got to act like a lady?"

Holden laughed and walked up the steps to where she was and sat, pulling her down beside of him and looked out toward the road Laurel had left on. "Thing is, Alex, as much as I'd like to keep you with me until I'm old and gray, there will be a time when you have to make a life for yourself. You'll want a family of your own."

She gasped. "I ain't gettin' married!"

"So you say." Holden grinned and ignored her outrage. "You'll find a man who will love you, even with you spitting and cussing and beating him up once a week, but finding him will be easier if you look and act like a lady."

Alex sighed. "You're gonna make me dress like a girl, ain't ya?"

Holden wrapped his arm around her shoulder and squeezed her to him. "You knew it would happen someday, Alex." He placed a kiss to the top of her head. "With Miss Montgomery new to town, I have to do what I can to make sure she doesn't run off like the last teacher did. They're too hard to come by way out here." Not that he'd ever let Laurel leave now that he'd found her again. He intended to keep her whether she liked the idea or not. He smiled at the thought. "Besides," he said, "she seemed pretty nice to me. I think if you start behaving, you'll see she isn't as bad as you think she is. You might even like her given enough time."

His daughter turned her head and looked up at him, her eyes narrowed a fraction. "What I got to like her for?"

"I didn't say you had to." Holden raised a hand and scratched his jaw. Alex was still staring up at him and he smiled before giving her a wink. "Just don't dislike her because she makes you do things you don't want to do."

"Did you like her?"

Holden's face heated and he hoped it didn't show. "Well, she can be a bit rude and comes off brash but I think she was just being that way because she was working. I figure she's quite nice when she don't have her teacher's hat on."

Alex squinted at him, her mouth forming a straight, hard line. "Don't you go getting sweet on her, pa. I can tell by the look in your eyes you liked her."

The heat on his face increased, traveled to his neck and landed around his heart. "What if she was sweet on me, instead?"

A horrified expression covered her face, her eyes widening. "Having her for my teacher is bad enough. I don't ever want to see her at my house again. Don't you dare get any ideas of courtin' her, pa. I won't have it."

Ideas of doing that very thing flitted through his mind but he didn't say as much. He left Alex there on the porch after giving her extra chores for misbehaving at school and walked back to the pasture, his thoughts on Laurel and what the other men in town would do once they got a look at her. He saw them lining up at her door, flowers in hand and slobbery smiles on their faces. His heart thumped harder the more the scene materialized in his mind's eye. One would have to be a complete fool to pass up a chance to court her and every man in town would be fighting for her hand once they got a good look at her.

Stopping by the fence he was repairing, he turned to look toward the road. Laurel was a sight for sore eyes and heaven knew he hadn't seen anything so pleasing since his brothers all showed up with their new wives on their arms. It was his turn. He wasn't the superstitious sort but having Laurel show up in Willow Creek couldn't be anything but fate. He was meant to have her and he would. He'd waited too damn long as it was and Alex might be against the idea but he couldn't stop thinking about it. One way or another, Laurel Montgomery would be his wife and he didn't have time to waste making it happen. He'd have to act fast and wondered how long he should wait before letting his intentions to court her be known.

CHAPTER 2

He wouldn't court that woman if she was the last available one in all of Montana.

Holden barely refrained from yelling, biting his tongue instead as Laurel gave him a disapproving look and talked down to him as if he was one of her unruly pupils.

He'd thought showing up early to pick up Alex, and have a chance to talk with Laurel was a good idea until she began berating him for disturbing her class, giving Alex ample excuse to act up and get away with it. Having to agree to allow Alex to be detained after school for her behavior was nearly too much, especially when his daughter glared at him nonstop.

"She can't hit people the way she does, regardless of what is said."

He blinked when he realized she was still talking. "What?"

She sighed and crossed her arms under her breasts. "Have you not heard a word I've said?"

In truth, he hadn't. Well, not much, anyway. He was too busy admiring her small waist and the way the yellow fabric of her dress made her whiskey colored eyes shine more brightly. The way her dark hair curled around her face, drawing his attention to lips so plump they just begged to be kissed.

And how much she apparently loathed the sight of him regardless of the way she'd acted back in Missoula. The look in her eyes told him that much. She wasn't happy to see him at all. "I heard most of it," he lied. He glanced over her shoulder, peering into the schoolhouse and watched Alex wash the blackboard, fury evident on her face. He locked eyes with Laurel again, saw the disregard she had for him, and the anger he felt chased all thoughts of wanting her away and told him to just leave. To let her be and his desire for her would diminish. "I've got a few things to take care of in town. I'll be back for Alex in a little bit."

He turned and left Laurel standing there, gape-mouthed. She wasn't through berating him, apparently. He ignored her exasperated gasp and the repeated use of his name and walked down the steps, exited the schoolyard and was headed toward the saloon at a fast clip. He needed a drink.

The Diamond Back Saloon was fairly active for a Monday. The noise inside was filled with men cussing and the occasional hoot of laughter. Holden wondered why there were so many people milling about so early in the day. He didn't have to guess long. The words, Laurel and pretty little thing, reached him before he'd made it to the bar.

"Afternoon, Holden. What's it going to be?"

He nodded his head at Vern, the bartender, and ordered whiskey. The glass was sat in front of him and he stood there staring at the amber liquid debating on drinking it. The stuff Vern sold was bad on the worst of days and downing the stuff was done with courage and puffed up pride. None of which he had today. Laurel had taken that from him the moment she set eyes on him.

"She got to you too, didn't she?"

Turning to look down the bar, Holden watched the men as they laughed. "She who?"

"The new schoolmarm. Laurel Montgomery."

He tried not to react but something on his face must have given him away. The men laughed again, raised their glasses before hooting and hollering and swilled their liquor before asking for another.

"She's a piece of work, I hear," Vern said as he refilled their glasses. "Mean and spiteful." He turned to look at him once he'd finished. "One would think a woman that fetching would have a sweet sort of disposition but I'm not sure she has it in her. She's just plain mean."

He smiled. "So it wasn't just me?"

The laughter returned. "No. She's a right ornery woman from what I've heard. Doesn't take too kindly to men, either." Vern grinned and nodded toward Ben Atwater. "What was it she said to you, Ben?"

Ben belched and tossed back his drink before turning to look down the bar. "She said I was a foul smelling sot and I should go drink off my stupor." He scowled and banged his glass on the top of the bar. "Wouldn't even take the flowers I found on the side of the road." He snorted. "As if I'd want to court a woman who was offended I drink. Why, she's too opinionated to ever get a husband, let alone keep one. It's probably why she's here! She's just a bitter old spinster no one wanted."

The gaggle of men inside the bar comforted Ben, telling him how wrong the schoolmarm was and Holden smiled as he listened to them. He wasn't about to agree. For all Laurel's faults, she was at least honest. Ben Atwater was the biggest drunk from here to Missoula.

His confrontation with Laurel was still fresh on his mind. He wasn't sure where he'd gone wrong, or what caused her to be so cross with him. He'd waited until the children were dismissed and were gathering their things before approaching her and the flower he'd picked up by the fence hadn't made her eyes sparkle like he thought it would. It had infuriated her. She'd torn into him immediately, giving the kids ample time to start misbehaving, Alex being the one to instigate it all, and within minutes, he'd been scolded and put in his place, all his hopes of courting, and then making Laurel his wife, dashed in an instant.

She apparently hated him.

It took him near half an hour to finish his drink, the laughter and the rude comments about Laurel remained the topic of conversation. Holden checked the time and said his goodbyes, laughing as the men continued to debate Laurel's less than appealing attributes and he almost wished he didn't have to face her again. As much as she heated his blood and made him think things he shouldn't about her, the venom she spouted was disheartening.

As badly as he wanted a wife, and a mother for Alex, he wasn't about to be saddled with a hateful woman, regardless of how pretty she was. There was only so much a man could put up with and even though bedding Laurel had been the single most exciting night he could remember in years, the moment she opened her mouth to berate him for something, what little desire he had for her would be gone.

He readjusted his hat, looked toward the school and felt a bit of hope stir in his chest when he saw Alex. He wouldn't have to face Laurel after all.

Alex ran across the street and was near breathless when she stopped in front of him. "Pa, I swear, I'll run away from home if I have to go back to class tomorrow."

Holden laughed and laid his hand on her shoulder as they walked down the street. "It wasn't that bad, was it?"

Her face twisted into a grimace. "She made us all switch seats and she sat me right in front of Jesse Samuels! That boy is a pest from the other side of the room. Now, he's right behind me."

"That doesn't sound too bad. Just don't turn around and you'll never even know he's there."

"That's what you think." Alex huffed out a breath and shook

her head. "She also told everyone in class my name was Alexandra and from this day on, they had to call me that. Jesse spent the rest of the day pulling my hair and saying Alexandra every other sentence."

Holden bit his lip to keep from grinning. They walked all the way to the brand new hotel before he stopped and looked down at his daughter. "Well, it is the name your mamma gave ya."

The fury shining in her eyes dimmed a bit. "I didn't ever say I hated the name. I just prefer Alex better."

He smiled and tossed her pigtails over her shoulders. "Well, why don't we just let Miss Montgomery have her way at school and we'll keep calling you Alex when you're not there. How's that?"

She sighed, tilted her head a bit as if thinking and finally nodded. "As long as everyone knows that outside of school, I'm Alex."

They entered the newly built hotel, greeted Joseph Brighton, the owner, as he said hello before they turned, heading to the restaurant. They'd made it a regular Monday ritual of having an early supper when the new hotel was built and so far, Alex had enjoyed her time alone with him.

They were seated, handed menus with the day's special and had ordered before Alex sighed. Holden looked up, noticed the look on her face and knew, there was something she wasn't telling him. He crossed his arms on the top of the table and just waited.

"Nobody likes her."

Holden didn't comment. It was pointless to debate the issue when he knew his daughter was probably right, especially after hearing what the men at the saloon had to say about Laurel.

She looked up at him before lowering her gaze. "Benjamin Atwater called her a shrew today. He said that's what his pa said she was. A hateful, dried out old shrew with no heart and she heard him. And you know what she did, pa?"

He shook his head. "No."

Alex looked almost remorseful as she sat back in her seat. "She looked like he'd thrown a rock at her head. Her eyes got all glassy like she was about to cry and then she just smiled and pretended he'd never said it, even though everyone was laughing at her."

Holden stared at his daughter as heat crawled up his neck. The conversation he'd heard earlier in the saloon came back to mind and he wondered how many others would be so bold as to tell Laurel what they thought of her. His own anger at her diminished, remorse filling him as he thought of her and how she'd feel knowing she was disliked. Knowing that he'd had ill thoughts about her, too.

If what Alex said was true, then it just proved Laurel did have a heart. It might have been black and shriveled to the size of a prune for some unknown reason but she did get her feelings hurt.

He sat back and thought of the conversations he'd had with her. She'd been very straight forward at the ranch and here in town, hadn't cracked a smile and had looked very stern, but he didn't miss the pink tint her cheeks took on when she first saw him. Or the way she avoided looking at him if she could. How straight her spine was, as if facing him was the hardest thing she'd ever had to do.

No one really knew her. Hell, he didn't for that matter. Their night together was about pleasure. They hadn't talked much once he entered her hotel room and he had no inkling of what circumstance brought her to Willow Creek. She may act like a spiteful woman who wanted nothing to do with him, but was she really?

Their food arrived and he watched Alex dig into her fried chicken while he sat there wondering what it was exactly that made Laurel act so bitter. It had to be something. Women didn't snap like she did without cause and he'd done nothing to offend her which made him think that someone, somewhere, knew why she had such a sour disposition. He knew just who to ask about it, too. His brother, Morgan, would be able to find out. There wasn't a person alive who could escape his scrutiny.

Making a mental note to talk to Morgan, he looked down at his plate, the meatloaf still slightly sizzling while his thoughts whirled. Laurel Montgomery was an enigma to everyone in town but one way or another, he'd find out what caused her to be so surly.

SHE'D SURVIVED another day of class but still felt the cold rush of fear skating down her spine. The kids, and the people in town, seemed to dislike her more than she'd hoped they would. She bolted the front door of the school house and walked back across the space, entering the small room behind it that was now her new home. It was sparsely furnished. A bed, a table with two chairs, a stove for cooking and a wardrobe for her belongings.

As rooms went, it was better than most boarding houses she'd found herself in. It was private, it didn't smell and the colorful rag-rug on the wood floor gave it a cheery feel.

So why did she feel so much misery while in it?

Filling the teapot with water, she checked the stove, adding more wood to the burning embers and waited for the fire to grow enough to boil her water. She looked at the foodstuff she had, debated on going to the hotel for supper and felt her stomach clench just thinking about it. She wasn't prepared to suffer through that humiliation again. Not yet. Being served by people who obviously didn't like her was embarrassing, especially when the other diners stared at her. No, she'd make due with what she had and not step back into that restaurant until she had no choice.

When her water had boiled, she poured it into her teapot, added the tea leaves and waited for it to steep while grabbing one of the three china cups she owned. Sitting at the small table, her

LILY GRAISON

thoughts a jumble of what ifs, she waited until the tea had turned dark and rich and the aroma filled her a bit with tranquility. Tea didn't cure all the troubles she had but at the moment, it chased away the most depressing.

Being in a town where no one liked her was soul crushing but she'd made her choice. She'd have to see it through. She just wished Holden Avery hadn't graced her door. For the first time in over a year she had thoughts she never dreamed of having about a man again. Thoughts that caused her face to heat, her stomach to clench delightfully and made her pulse beat so fast, she could hear the blood racing in her ears.

She sighed, added a bit of sugar to her tea and took a sip while trying to clear her head. Regardless of her feelings where Holden Avery was concerned, she'd stick to the plan. No man was worth the pain they brought, especially one as handsome as Holden Avery. If being hateful to every person she came into contact with, even him, was what it took to protect her heart, then so be it. Living out her life alone was a lonely proposition but it was one she could live with. She hoped.

CHAPTER 3

GREETING her students as they ran up the steps of the schoolhouse was done with as stern a look as possible. It almost killed her not to smile at them and say how happy she was for them to be back. Truth was, she adored kids and teaching was probably as close as she'd ever get to having children of her own.

She sighed, the noise from the school bell ringing inside her head incessantly as Jesse continued to ring it without fail. Seeing no one else running toward the school, she was just about to turn when she saw the horse, and the small rider seated in front of her father. Laurel's pulse leaped when she recognized Holden and Alexandra coming down the road.

Of all the people she hadn't wanted to see, it was him. Her heart nearly beat out of control whenever she looked at the man and she hated the effect he had on her.

She'd sworn off men after being lied to and played for a fool, and knew the only way to be happy in life was to make her own decisions. And she had. Life would have worked out fine had she not made the grave mistake of falling for a handsome face back in Missoula. Now, she was stuck in a town with that same man. A man who heated her blood beyond reason and brought to mind images of them together she couldn't seem to forget.

Sighing, she waited for Alexandra to dismount and prayed Holden wouldn't follow his daughter to the building. Her prayers weren't usually answered and today was no different. She tried to ignore him as he walked toward her. Tried to be indifferent to his chiseled features, the whiskers on his chin where he'd not bothered to shave or the sparkling blue eyes that were firmly latched on her.

She lowered her arms when he climbed the steps, looked only at Alexandra and hoped he'd just go away.

He didn't.

"I think we got off on the wrong foot, Miss Montgomery." He smiled, and lifted his hand, the largest red apple she'd ever seen resting on his palm.

Her pulse leaped and she cursed her traitorous heart for even noticing the man. "An apple for the teacher." She looked up, gave him a blank look and sighed. "How very... typical."

She turned, walked into the classroom and shut the door behind her, leaving Holden on the front stoop while her heart stammered away in her chest. She crossed the room, stepped behind her desk and inhaled deeply, telling herself it was okay to be so rude to Holden, that if she wasn't, he'd never leave her alone.

Picking up her lesson book, she flipped to today's lessons, scanning what she'd written for each age group and lifted her head to look at her class just as the door to the classroom opened. Her heart skipped a beat as she saw Holden framed in the doorway, looking as handsome and strong as he always did, that blasted smirk on his face. This man would be the death of her.

He crossed the room, his gaze locked on her, and stopped in front of her desk. "Your fancy words and hateful attitude won't make me go away, Laurel." He leaned toward her, his words a bare whisper. "If nothing else, they amuse me." He sat the apple in front of her, grinning up at her as he leaned back. "Have a good day. I'll see you this afternoon."

The sound of his boots hitting the floor as he walked away echoed in her head. The light from the open door dimmed as he shut it behind him.

The man obviously wasn't about to give up. Apparently she wasn't rude enough. She had to dissuade him from pursuing her but how? He was obviously stubborn to the core but so was she. She'd chased off more men than her father could parade in front of her and a cowboy in the middle of nowhere wouldn't get the best of her. She wouldn't allow it.

It was several minutes before she was able to focus on her class. When she looked up, everyone was staring at her, one face in particular catching her attention. Alexandra Avery looked madder than a wet hen and if Laurel had to guess, she'd say it was because of her father. He was obviously trying to court her and his daughter knew it. And didn't like it one bit.

Ignoring them all, she turned her attention back to her lesson plan and tried to overlook the flutter in her chest every time she looked at that apple.

☊

HOLDEN WALKED INTO THE JAILHOUSE. Morgan dropped the papers in his hand and looked up as Holden shut the front door. His brother shook his head and leaned back in his chair. "If you're here to complain about the new school teacher, I've heard it all already."

"Steady complaints about her then?"

"You wouldn't believe it." Morgan grinned and crossed his arms over his chest. "Ben wanted me to arrest her for calling him a drunk."

Holden laughed and grabbed the chair across from Morgan's

desk, turning it backwards and straddled the seat. "Can't arrest people for speaking the truth."

"No, you can't." Leaning forward, Morgan laid his arms across his desk. "So, what brings you by?"

"Laurel Montgomery."

Morgan laughed. "Why am I not surprised?"

"She's hiding something." When his brother lifted one eyebrow, Holden knew he was intrigued. "Don't you find it peculiar she's so... ornery?"

"Not really. A lot of people are. Take Edna Pierce for example."

They shared a laugh before sobering. "She doesn't look old enough to be as bitter as she is. What do you know about her?"

"Nothing much." Morgan stood, picked up the papers on his desk and tossed them into the stove. "Comes from somewhere in Arizona, I think."

"You think?" Holden shifted in his seat. "Can you find out for sure?"

Morgan gave him a curious look. "Why?"

Holden shrugged his shoulder. "No reason."

His brother laughed as he picked up his hat, placing it on his head. "You're a terrible liar, Holden. I can see it in your eyes." He walked around the desk and motioned to the door. "Come walk the town with me and you can tell me all about Laurel Montgomery. I'm sure you know more than any other man in town does."

"What makes you think that?"

Morgan stopped, turned his head to Holden and stared at him for long moments before grinning. "I actually didn't but the look on your face tells me you do. Is there something you're not telling me?"

"No." Holden wondered if Morgan could see the lie on his face. He stared him in the eye and kept on talking, ignoring the accusation. "I just know she's mean spirited, loathes the sight of me and makes me think things no decent man should think about a woman."

"You and half the men in town." Morgan shut the door on the jail and readjusted his gun belt. "Seems to me the man who can withstand that waspish tongue of hers will be the one who impresses the lady first and something tells me you're just the man to do it. Lord knows you're used to rejection."

Holden smirked at his brother. "Not my fault all the available women who come through here always find out I'm here after they made the grave mistake of taking up with the wrong characters. Speaking of, how's Abigail and the baby?"

They talked about nonsensical things as Morgan made his rounds through town. Their last stop was the Diamond Back Saloon and once inside the talk was the same as it usually was now. Laurel Montgomery.

SHE JUST COULDN'T ESCAPE the man. Laurel hid her face behind the restaurant menu and hoped they hadn't seen her. Alexandra was talking a mile a minute and her voice carried as if the child were screaming and so far, Holden only had eyes for his daughter.

Hearing the sound of chairs scraping across the wooden floor, Laurel peeked over the top of her menu. Her exhaled breath caused the menu in her hand to sway when she saw them taking a seat near the front of the restaurant. They hadn't seen her after all.

Pushing her embarrassment aside, she'd had no choice but come to the restaurant. If she had to eat one more meal alone, she'd hurt someone. Coming to the hotel was still disconcerting. No one bothered to speak to her, which was fine by her, but the looks they gave her as they ate, their whispered words a hushed murmur in the background, was just too much most days.

She was used to crowds of people. Had spent her life being the center of attention but look at her now. Reduced to sitting alone in a restaurant while the other patrons whispered about her and made no secret she was the topic of their conversations.

The server came back to her table and Laurel smiled at her. The dire faced woman didn't return the gesture. She stared at her unmoving and Laurel placed her order, reluctantly gave the menu back and sighed.

This town had to be home to the most unfriendly group of people she'd ever met. Not that she'd helped matters any with the way she acted toward everyone, but still. She wondered if acting so off-putting was as smart as she'd thought. It drew attention to her like nothing else did, apparently, and the last thing she needed was more attention.

Draping her napkin across her lap, Laurel made the mistake of lifting her head and looking across the restaurant again. Holden was staring at her, that irritating smirk on his face. She felt heat burn her face as she blushed before looking away.

A shadowy form appeared in the corner of her eye. Glancing up she saw Holden, standing now and crossing the room toward her. "Oh Lord," she whimpered, and busied herself looking into her reticule in order to ignore him.

"Laurel," he said, tipping his head toward her.

He'd removed his hat, his dark hair longer than most men she knew wore it. It hung nearly to his collar and framed his face perfectly. A face the man rarely shaved, she noticed. The whiskers of a growing beard shadowed his jaw line and accentuated his lips. His plain shirt was a bit snug and hugged his chest, hiding those dips and curves she remembered touching.

She blinked, reminded herself she wasn't getting involved with anyone in this town, and that included friendship, and lifted her chin, throwing him a disdainful look. "Holden. Are you lost?"

He grinned. "No. I just came to ask if you'd like to join us." He motioned to the table Alexandra was sitting at, the look on the child's face clearly saying she didn't share her father's good-natured sentiment.

Laurel threw him an aloof look, said, "No, thank you," and continued to rummage around in her bag.

He stood motionless for long moments before he leaned down, bracing one hand on the table, the other on the back of her chair and lowered his face next to her ear. "Ignore me all you want, woman, but I'm not leaving. I have every intention to make you my wife so you might as well face the fact and stop being so ornery toward me. I want you, Laurel, and I aim to have you."

He straightened, smiled down at her and turned and walked away.

Laurel gaped at his retreating back, his words whispering through her head like a sweet kiss on a hot, sultry night. Make her his wife? A shiver raced down her spine as images flooded her brain. Thoughts of being in that man's bed caused her breath to catch. Listening to his seductive voice every night as he took her body to heights she could only imagine and seeing his smiling face every morning when she woke.

A fine sheen of sweat broke out on her skin as he sat back down and looked her way. The desire in his eyes caused her pulse to leap.

She forced herself to look away. If she'd be true to her body's demands, she'd be tempted to just throw her reservations to the wind and see what sort of trouble she could make with him, wife or not. Lord knew they had no problem getting along in bed. That night they spent together came back to her on a daily basis and she was a woman who'd experienced more than most. Her shameful past would haunt her forever but there was nothing to be done about that now. She just had to accept her life as it was and make the best of what she had, stay hidden and try not to draw too much attention to herself in order to protect her whereabouts.

The server returned with her meal and it took everything in

her to concentrate enough to eat. She was half tempted to have it packaged to go but wasn't about to run to her little room in the back of the school house with her tail tucked. Especially not from a man. She didn't care how good-looking he was or how much her heart fluttered just looking at him.

Taking her time eating had been the plan, just so she'd have something to do besides stare at the same four walls of her room but those nervous butterflies in her stomach screamed disaster. She ate quickly, trying to not seem as if she was shoveling it in and was ready to go in record time. She stood, not waiting for the server to come back with her ticket and kept her eyes on the floor as she passed Holden Avery and his daughter. Holden's soft, "See you soon, Miss Montgomery," was ignored and it wasn't until she'd paid for her food and was outside on the wooden sidewalk that she realized what a hypocrite she was.

She made the children in her classroom behave in a certain manner. They were to say thank you when appropriate, greet others with courtesy and treat everyone they met as they too would like to be treated. As of yet, she hadn't lived by her words. She acted in the complete opposite manner. She was rude, met everyone who spoke with her in a brash manner and stuck her nose up at those who dared look upon her. All because the men in her short twenty-six years of life were controlling to the point of suffocation.

Slipping her straw hat on her head, she tied the ribbon under her chin, exhaling a deep breath before glancing back inside the restaurant window. Holden was staring at her and somehow she knew he would be. The man just didn't give up. His arrogant assumption that he'd marry her came to mind as she looked at him and she smiled before she could stop herself. She knew it was a mistake the moment his eyes lit up in reaction.

If only her circumstances were different. On one level, being married to a man like Holden Avery would be a dream come true for her, but she knew men to be lying and untrustworthy. He was probably no different. So what if a single glance made her heart race. Or remembering him in the altogether was enough to make her mouth water and want to beg for more. He was certainly a man any sane woman would want to know more about. Unfortunately, she wasn't just any woman. She didn't need or want a man in her life and that was a plan she intended to stick with.

Trying to forget her past, she gave Holden one last look before starting for the school. She'd only made it as far as the stagecoach station when Edna Pierce yelled her name.

"Miss Montgomery! I'd like a word with you."

Laurel sighed and stopped walking. She'd seen Edna on the other side of the road and had kept her head down, hoping the woman wouldn't see her.

Of all the people Laurel had met in Willow Creek, Edna was the one she avoided the most. The woman was just too irritating to carry on a civil conversation with. She gossiped too much and gave Laurel disapproving looks when the whispered secrets she loved sharing were met with silence.

Laurel folded her hands in front of her and waited for Edna to cross the street. She forced a smile onto her face as she reached her. As much as it pained her to be nice to the woman, having her as an enemy would be disastrous.

"Miss Montgomery," Edna said, breathless, "I wanted to formally invite you to the town festival that will be taking place a month from Saturday." Edna smiled and lifted her chin, a haughty look crossing her face. "We'll be raising funds for the new doctor we hope to attract and everyone will be participating. There will be picnics and dancing, games and auctions. It looks to be the event of the year."

"Oh. I'll help anyway I can, Mrs. Pierce, but a teacher's salary is very meager."

"Yes, I'm well aware of that, which is why I signed you up for the auction."

Laurel raised one eyebrow at her. "Excuse me?"

Edna smiled again, her chest puffed up arrogantly. "It was my idea, really. As a woman of standing in our community, and a member of the town council, I've been asked to oversee the entire affair and it wasn't hard to come up with an idea I knew would raise the most money. With so few women in Willow Creek, the men here in town, and the surrounding area, don't have the pleasure of sweet treats very often." Edna heaved a breath, her eyes twinkling as if she'd accomplished some great feat. "You'll need to prepare a confection for the auction. A cake or pie. Cookies if you prefer but the more appealing the treat, the more men will bid on it."

"Bid?"

"Yes, bid." Edna straightened her spine and gave her a disapproving look. "Goodness, Miss Montgomery, do you not listen?"

Laurel opened her mouth to respond but thought better of it. She'd been listening, and wasn't at all happy this woman had signed her up for something she wished to take no part in. "I don't do much baking, Mrs. Pierce. And actually, I'm sure I'll be too busy with lesson plans to attend this town festival."

Thoughts of mingling with the townsfolk set Laurel's teeth on edge. She avoided people most of the time but being forced to socialize with them… that would never do.

She smiled to lesson the blow. "I appreciate you including me but it wasn't necessary. I'll donate what funds I can for this new doctor but baking in order for someone to bid on my pie? I can't see how that will help you."

"Oh, pish-posh!" Edna said. "I've heard the rumors about your displeasing personality, dear, but trust me, once the gentlemen in the area get a chance to talk with you, they'll change their minds. Now, shall I put you down for a pie or for a cake?"

Laurel blinked. Was Edna Pierce daft or did she just not care about anyone's thoughts and feelings but her own? When the woman just stood there looking at her, Laurel realized it was the latter. What Edna wanted is what Edna got. She sighed. "I can bake a pie for you. Where shall I drop it off?"

Edna's smile lit her face. "Oh, just bring it to the clearing behind the mercantile on the first Saturday in September." She turned in a whirl of skirts, mumbling to herself and Laurel's eyes widened.

"Edna, I'll not be attending the festival!"

The woman raised her hand to wave, looked over her shoulder and smiled. "Of course you will, dear. Now, have a good evening!"

And with that, she was gone. Laurel stared after her for long minutes before she finally exhaled a deep breath.

As hard as she tried to not get involved with the people of this town, it was getting harder by the day. And now Edna had practically forced her to do so. Signing her up for something she had no intention of even attending.

She turned and resumed her walk back to the school house, her thoughts on how to get out of participating in the festival. The sound of a child talking caught her attention and she turned her head toward the street, her pulse leaping as she saw Holden and Alexandra on a black stallion headed out of town. As always, Holden smiled and tipped his hat to her. And just as she did every time she saw him, she tried to ignore those fluttering butterflies swimming in her stomach as she turned her head to look away from him.

CHAPTER 4

As LUCK WOULD HAVE IT, the first Saturday in September was as bright and cheery as they came. Laurel looked out the small window of her room and heaved a sigh. Why couldn't it have rained?

She turned to check her appearance in the small mirror hanging on the wall, tucked in a few errant strands of hair that refused to stay put and straightened the front of her dress. Dread settled in her stomach and the aroma of that apple pie she'd labored over all morning was making her queasy. She was going to have to take the thing across town regardless of her desire not to.

Just looking at the thing caused her stomach to quiver. Holden Avery had given her enough apples over the past month to fill several crusts but she'd purposely given every one of them away to one of her students just so she wouldn't be reminded of him. When she'd ventured to the mercantile for more, Mrs. Jenkins had informed her all the apples in her store had come from the Avery ranch.

She just couldn't escape the man.

Grabbing her pie, she slipped out the back door, securing it behind her and walked in a hurried pace to the clearing behind the mercantile. Her intentions were to leave the pie, let Edna know she was there, and slip away unseen.

Reaching the clearing, Laurel smiled. Her plan to slip away would be easy with so many people in the area. She stopped behind the store to get her bearings.

She hadn't realized there were so many people in and around the Willow Creek area and noticed a lot of the children from her classroom in attendance as she looked at those gathered.

The clearing had been raked free of the first leaves falling from the trees, garlands of late summer flowers and early fall blooms strung from the trees and tables, chairs, benches and long wooden tables covered in bright cloths made the entire area warm and inviting. Too bad she wasn't staying. It was sure to be fun.

Spotting a table on the left filled with cakes and pies, she headed in that direction, avoiding eye contact with everyone she passed.

One person in particular caught her attention as she neared the table. Alexandra Avery was screeching like a hellion and running around the table as if it weren't filled with food, but that wasn't what made Laurel stop. It was the pretty blue dress the girl was wearing. Her hair was flowing loose too, her blond locks curling at the ends and made her appear much older than she actually was.

The girl looked up at her and crossed her arms over her chest. "What are you doing here?"

Laurel squinted at her. "Don't worry, Alexandra, I won't be staying." The girl looked so happy, Laurel had half a mind to stay just to irritate her but seeing Alexandra meant her father was there somewhere and she'd been dutifully avoiding him for the last month. He was the last person she wished to see.

Setting her pie down on the table, Laurel took another glance at Alexandra. "You look very nice, Alexandra."

"Pft…" Alexandra made a face at her. "Pa bought me this frock and said I had to wear it. I'm guessing you're the reason why."

Laurel hid a smile. "I suggested you should look and behave like a lady, yes."

"I knew it." Alexandra huffed out a breath and shook her head. "Don't be thinking he'll do everything you say now. Only reason I didn't cause a fuss over it was because he said I looked like my momma all dressed up and he loves my momma." The girl eyed her with a calculating expression. "Pa said my momma was the prettiest woman in all of Willow Creek and they'll never be another like her."

"I'm sure there won't be."

Alexandra nodded her head. "So even if he goes out of his way to be nice to you, it don't mean nothing. He don't like ya. He probably just feels sorry for you, is all."

Laurel doubted that. Holden had made it perfectly clear what his intentions were and regardless of what Alexandra said, Laurel knew her father wouldn't stop trying to court her. She didn't know much about the man but stubborn stuck to some people like a bad haircut and Holden Avery was stubborn to his core.

Finished with their brief conversation, Alexandra left with a stiff nod of her head. Watching the girl walk away, Laurel knew Holden had to be in the clearing, somewhere, and she needed to find Edna, make her presence known, and leave before he spotted her.

She turned to look for Edna and saw her immediately, rushing about the clearing and issuing orders like a heavyset general to those following close behind her. Laurel sighed and headed toward her, intent on making her appearance known and then sneaking away.

"Laurel! I was just looking for you." Edna beamed as she came to a stop in front of her. "Did you remember to bring a confection for the auction?"

"Yes. I left it on the table." She forced a smile on her face and tried to remember to be polite. "You've done a nice job organizing everything, Edna. I'm sure the town is grateful."

Edna laughed, her eyes shining with delight. "Of course they are." She took Laurel's arm and turned, the women behind Edna's large frame all looking a bit haggard. "Ladies, I'm sure you all know Miss Montgomery, our new school teacher." When Edna turned her head to look at her again, Laurel knew getting away wouldn't be as easy as she'd hoped.

Introductions were made and after long minutes of greeting the other ladies responsible for making the festival run like clockwork, Laurel was ready to just be rude and excuse herself. She was saved from the embarrassing episode by a woman Laurel had seen around town, a petite woman with blond hair and an easy-going smile.

"Thank you, Edna, for introducing the ladies to Miss Montgomery, but I'm afraid I have to steal her away. I have things to discuss with her about teaching Elizabeth when she's old enough to start reading."

Edna's mouth opened and closed like a fish before the woman grabbed Laurel's arm and whisked them both away. When they stopped on the other side of the clearing, Laurel could only stare.

"Well, that was easier than I thought it would be." The woman laughed, holding out her hand. "I'm Abigail Avery, by the way. I don't think we've been formally introduced."

Avery? Laurel's stomach clenched tight. "Any relation to Holden and Alexandra?"

Abigail's beaming smile lit her entire face. "I'm married to Holden's brother, Morgan, the marshal here in Willow Creek."

"I see." Laurel wondered if Holden had sent his sister-in-law over to her in hopes she could persuade her into seeing his finer qualities. She'd already seen most of them, she was sure, but that didn't mean she wanted to hear more. The less she thought of Holden, the better off she was.

Glancing across the clearing to where Edna still stood, Laurel watched her before saying, "Do you think she'll notice if I'm not here?"

Abigail laughed. "Oh, she'll know, trust me, so don't get any ideas of sneaking away. If I have to suffer and be made to stay, so do you."

They made their way back to the dessert table where Laurel had sat her pie and just seeing it there made her cringe. Baking wasn't something she'd spent much time doing but thankfully her pie looked edible. She noticed the name cards beside each dessert, the name of the lady who'd baked it proudly displayed and her eyes widened. "I wasn't aware everyone would know who baked what."

Abigail nodded. "It's Edna's way of showing her superiority. Everyone knows her cakes are the best in town and the price she'll get from hers will cause her ego to grow three sizes." She laughed and fingered a few of the name tags, looking to see who had made what, Laurel supposed. "Which one is yours?"

Laurel wanted to refuse to answer but saw no reason to do so. Edna would be sure to make a fuss because it wasn't tagged and Abigail would find out anyway. "This one," she said, pointing it out.

"Oh, that looks fabulous." Abigail looked around the dish before saying, "You didn't tag it as yours?"

"No."

"Well, let's just fix that, shall we?"

Laurel sighed as Abigail took one of the small slips of paper, wrote Laurel Montgomery on it and propped it against the side of her pie. She glanced around the clearing again, noticed the men looking at that dessert table with hungry eyes and knew Edna had been right. The money they'd raise from the baking auction would help them raise the funds they needed to attract a new doctor but as she looked back at her pie, Laurel couldn't help feeling embarrassed by it. When the men in town heard she'd made that pie, the silence that followed the bidding for it would be eerie.

HOLDEN SAW her standing near the baked goods table with Abigail and wasn't sure who to thank for that small blessing, his sister-in-law or Laurel for even showing up.

When he'd heard of the festival, he knew he'd have the perfect opportunity to talk to Laurel without her shooing him out of her classroom or walking past him in the street as if he didn't exist. He wasn't even sure why he bothered anymore. The woman obviously didn't like him, regardless of the time they spent together in Missoula.

Her disdain where he was concerned didn't make him want to stop trying though.

If it hadn't been for Alex, he would have already been at Laurel's door trying to woo her but his daughter's adamant refusal to like the woman had halted those plans. He couldn't make Alex like her and courting the woman would only cause problems in the future. Which left him staring at her from afar and watching to see if anyone else in town could break through her icy exterior and actually get her to talk.

"I don't care how much you stare at her, Holden, she won't walk over here and start a conversation with you."

Holden grinned and turned to look at his twin brother, Colt. "She wouldn't come over to talk to me even if you paid her."

"Well, she's smart." Colt laughed and crossed his arms over his chest. "Any woman willing to talk to you would make me think they were daft."

"Oh, she's smart all right. And hiding something."

Colt raised one eyebrow at him. "You're getting as suspicious as Morgan now. Everyone he meets, he thinks they're hiding something."

"Most people are."

"Really?" Colt grinned. "And what are you hiding?"

Holden gave him a sideways glance, one corner of his mouth slanting up. "None of your business."

Edna interrupted their conversation when she gave an unladylike whistle and gained everyone's attention. She made a boring speech, gloated about how wonderful the festival was turning out, thanks to her efforts, and mentioned the number of activities that would be taking place throughout the day. The dance planned for later that night had everyone in good spirits, himself included, as long as one spiteful little schoolmarm was planning on being in attendance.

The auctions started and everyone seemed to congregate in one general area. Directly in front of him. He lost sight of Laurel in the rush and craned his neck to try and find her. It was hopeless. There were too many people gathered to spot her.

The cake auction went about as fast as he thought it would and he waited, listening to every lady's name called as her cake or pie was offered and it wasn't until that last plate was lifted that he smiled. An apple pie, baked by the new school teacher herself. The fact she'd baked apple pie amused him. He'd given her enough over the last month to bake a half a dozen pies.

Edna started the bidding and the silence that followed was astounding. Holden watched the faces of the men around him and they all seemed to be looking at their feet. That's when he realized why Laurel had looked so forlorn when she'd looked at that table of desserts. She'd known this would happen.

Movement out of the corner of his eye caught his attention. The summer yellow of Laurel's dress drawing notice. She was walking between the mercantile and the telegraph office at a fast clip. He watched her disappear around the corner before looking back at Edna. The disapproving look on the woman's face said it all. She wasn't any more pleased with the silence than he was.

He lifted his hand, drawing her attention and she smiled,

raising the bid price. No one spoke but several people turned to look at him. Then someone from the front of the crowd matched the bid until it was raised again.

The bidding war began and Holden couldn't have been happier.

LAUREL LOOKED up from the book she was reading when someone knocked on her door. Dread settled like a weight in her stomach. It was probably Edna, come to berate her for sneaking off from the festival.

She sighed and debated on just not answering but she knew the woman wouldn't go away. Standing, she laid her book down and crossed the room and opened the door.

Seeing Holden Avery standing there didn't surprise her much either. He'd never knocked on her door but she knew it was only a matter of time.

He smiled and Laurel had to force herself not to return the gesture. "Are you lost?"

"No, ma'am." He thumbed up the front of his hat and gave her a look that said he knew he wasn't welcome at her door and was choosing to ignore it. "Abigail and Sarah packed a picnic lunch enough to feed half the town. We'll be taking it out by the creek. Just wanted to know if you'd like to join us."

Her pulse leaped. He was asking her to a picnic? The sincere look in his eyes and that handsome smile on his face caused that small voice in the back of her mind to scream, yes. It begged her to accept. To not worry about her stupid reservations for once. To just go spend the day with this man, who obviously went out of his way to try and talk to her, but the thought of doing it sent fear coursing through her body. She couldn't get attached to this man, no matter how much she wanted to. "Thank you for the offer, but I must decline."

He gave her a slight nod of his head, the smile that had been on his face dimming just a fraction. "Somehow I knew you were going to say that."

"Yet you still found your way to my door to ask. Why?"

The smile remained and filled his blue eyes, the mingled greens and purple catching her attention. "Can't blame a man for trying."

"I don't suppose you can but it really is pointless, I can assure you."

He blinked up at her, bid her a good day, and it wasn't until he left her standing there on the back porch steps of the school house, alone, that she realized how utterly miserable her life was.

And she only had one person to thank for that.

Thinking of him, she sighed and walked back into her little room, looking at the bleak walls.

Why had her life turned out to be so dire? She'd had such high hopes for her future a year ago. Now she was reduced to being rude to people who, in other circumstances, she would have enjoyed talking to, and living out her days in silence while trapped within four walls of a schoolhouse in order to protect her heart.

This wasn't living. It was existing and somehow it didn't seem to be the answer to all her prayers like she thought it would be. Instead, it was the very worst of hell.

Add in the fact that Holden Avery was the most tempting thing she'd seen in ages. Thoughts of him plagued her every moment of the day and the misery piled on until she felt as if she was drowning.

Something had to change. She'd tried, honestly tried to set a course for her life but one reckless night in Missoula had changed all her carefully laid out plans. She couldn't ignore Holden regardless of how much she tried so why was she still trying? She liked the man, aggravating as he was at times, and memories of him caused her to lay awake more than one night with her body aching for his touch.

But was that reason enough to lay all her plans aside? To spend her life as a spinster and die at a ripe old age, pleased with herself because she'd done exactly what she wanted to do, not something a man told her she had to do?

She sighed. It was too confusing to think about. Her heart and head needed to act as one but her heart was screaming the loudest at the moment. She needed to make a decision and stick with it but what if she chose the wrong path?

CHAPTER 5

HOLDEN SAW her when he turned the wagon and started for the other end of the street. She was standing in front of the schoolhouse, a straw hat in one hand while she draped a shawl over her shoulders. She was staring at him, the look on her face telling him she was trying to decide if turning around would be the better option.

He smiled and pulled the reins when he neared her, the horses stopping and giving Alexandra time to start protesting. "Why does she have to come along, pa? I don't want to spend the day with her."

When they came to a complete stop, he ignored Alex, set the brake with his foot and jumped to the ground before crossing the road. "I hope this means you've changed your mind." Laurel's cheeks turned a pretty shade of pink and he felt his pulse leap at the sight of it.

"Don't read more into this than there is." She glanced up at him, her cheeks darkening. "I'm just bored is all."

Holden grinned. He didn't care what her excuse was, as long as he got to spend the day with her, he'd let her make up any ole' lie she felt like telling.

He offered her his arm and walked her back across the street, lifted her into the wagon and gave Alex a look that spoke volumes. His daughter's mouth tightened into a thin white line, her eyes narrowing to show her displeasure and he ignored it, climbed up into the seat and had the horses moving again before his pulse stopped racing.

They rode in silence until they reached the prairie and ventured off the main road. He followed behind Morgan and Abigail's wagon as they jostled across the yellowing autumn grass. His father's shock of white hair glinted in the sun as he sat in the back of Morgan's wagon and when he turned his head to look back at them, Laurel asked, "Who is that?"

"My father." He saw her look at him out of the corner of his eye and smiled. "His name is James but don't worry about trying to talk to him. Chances are he wouldn't hear you."

"Is he deaf?"

"No." Holden shook his head and gave the reins another small tug to get the horses to turn toward the creek. "He's sick. We're not really sure what's wrong with him but he keeps to himself most of the time. Talks to people no one can see and pretty much tunes the rest of us out."

She turned to look at the wagon in front of them, back at his father, and Holden glanced over at her. The sun made those whiskey colored eyes shine, her complexion, flawless. Small tendrils of hair had escaped the confines of the bun she'd pulled it all into and those stray curls kissed her cheek, sweeping low to tease her lips.

They reached the creek and Alex wasted no time jumping from the back of the wagon and running toward the thin ribbon of water winding its way through the trees. She was shucking her boots as Holden jumped to the ground and turned to help Laurel down.

He reached up, placing his hands about her small waist and she stared up at him when her feet touched the ground. Just being this close to her again sent waves of need through him. The tantalizing scent of roses filled the air and he remembered their one night together, of burying his face into the curve of her neck and finding that tantalizing aroma there. How he'd wanted to drown in it and couldn't pass by his mother's rose garden without being reminded of Laurel. He stared down at her. His gaze traveled her face and if they hadn't been surrounded by his family, he would have kissed those raspberry lips until she begged him to stop.

He tightened his hold on her briefly before reluctantly letting go of her. Glancing over at Morgan and Abigail, he saw them both grinning at him. Inviting Laurel to the picnic had been their idea. He'd agreed with them until he found himself walking to the schoolhouse. Laurel refusing him hadn't come as a surprise and he'd be lying if he said her initial refusal hadn't torn at his heart a bit. The pain didn't last long though. Not once he saw her by the road, nervously looking his way.

She turned away from him and walked toward the creek and Holden watched her until Morgan walked over to him and laughed.

"I never thought I'd see the day you'd go all moon-eyed over a woman."

"You forget I was married once."

"No, I haven't." Morgan reached around him and lifted the blankets from the back of the wagon. "I know you loved Maggie but trust me when I say, you never looked at her like you do that little schoolmarm."

Holden watched Morgan walk back to Abigail, his words whispering inside his head. His brother was right. He had loved Maggie, had the first time he saw her, but it felt different from what he felt for Laurel. He wasn't sure why but as he turned his head to look over at her, his body tightened, his pulse leaped and he knew he'd do anything to win her heart.

"You are such a fool." Laurel sighed at her own whispered words. She'd walked away from Holden with her heart in her throat. The way he'd looked at her when he lifted her down from the wagon sent chills racing up and down her spine and if they'd been alone, she was positive he would have kissed her.

And she would have let him.

She still wasn't sure why she'd even stepped out of the school-house and accompanied him on the picnic. Common sense told her to leave him be, to ignore him and he'd eventually leave her alone. But that secret place in her heart, the one that craved the sight of him, wouldn't let her.

As much as she hated to admit it, she looked forward to seeing him everyday. Just looking into those so-blue eyes caused her pulse to race. To see him smile at her like he had secrets he wanted to share sent her heart soaring and her thoughts racing.

And she was powerless to do anything about it.

She stopped by the bank of the creek, turning to look at Alexandra. She was in the water to her knees, the hem of her dress swaying in the current. The need to tell her to get out of the water, that it was too late in the year to be wading in the creek was strong but she ignored it. The child despised her and wouldn't appreciate being told what to do outside of school. The fact her father had asked her along for the picnic was upsetting to the girl enough as it was. She'd seen the look on Alexandra's face when she reached the wagon. She hadn't been the least bit happy. Laurel couldn't really blame her. She probably wouldn't have wanted her teacher along for a family outing either, especially one her father seemed to spend his time trying to talk to.

Alexandra turned to look at her as if she could hear Laurel's thoughts. Laurel stared at her, her facial expression passive. Alexandra's blond curls swayed in the breeze and Laurel knew with just a glance, the girl took her looks after her mother. She shared none of the dark looks her father had, except for the blue of her eyes. When Alexandra didn't move, or blink, but continued to stare at her, Laurel sighed. "It's rude to stare, Alexandra."

"I know. My pa told me that years ago." She turned and started out of the water, climbing onto the bank, the hem of her dress dragging on the ground and collecting bits of grass and dirt. When she stood on solid ground, she lifted her chin, her eyes narrowed. "You like my pa, don't ya?"

Laurel wasn't sure how to answer. "Define like."

Alexandra lifted one eyebrow. "You want him to court you?"

"No." There, the first question she'd been asked where she could give an honest answer. "Why do you ask?"

"'Cause I think he wants to court you."

He wants more than that, Laurel thought to herself. Thinking of him saying he intended on marrying her caused her heart to slam against her ribcage and those butterflies in her stomach danced in erratic patterns until she felt dizzy. That little voice in her head she'd been trying to ignore, yelled at her to let Holden know it was okay to come calling on her and that she'd be waiting with bated breath until he did.

Laurel blinked instead and chased the thoughts away, choosing to ignore his whispered admission. "What makes you think that?"

"'Cause he's always looking at ya. He goes all funny too. He don't listen to me when I talk and when he does answer, he makes no sense."

"That doesn't mean he wants to court me, Alexandra. Maybe he's just preoccupied."

She shook her head, her curls bouncing across her shoulders. "No, he likes you. I can tell. He's never courted a woman and as far as I know, he don't go near the saloon and those women who live there and I know from what my uncle Tristan told me that every man wants a wife. So my pa likes you all right but what I want to know is, if he tried to court you, would you let him."

Laurel stared at Alexandra and the first answer to pop into her head was, yes. She shook her head and said, "No," instead. "I have no desire to court anyone so rest assured, you'll not have to worry about me being any part of your life other than the few hours you spend in my classroom."

Alexandra stared at her for long minutes, nodding her head after finding Laurel's answer sufficient. "Good, 'cause you're all wrong for my pa. He needs a woman who isn't mean. My ma was as sweet as a flower and my pa loved her with all his heart. Why, I think that's why he ain't never remarried. He can't find another woman as pretty and sweet as she was."

"You're probably right."

Alexandra gave her one last look and took off running toward the wagons. Another was coming across the prairie and Laurel watched the man and woman in the seat while Alexandra's words rattled around in her head.

The girl didn't like her, which was obvious, but knowing Holden had never courted since his wife's death was intriguing. She couldn't help but wonder why. Had he without Alexandra's knowledge?

She thought back to the night they shared in Missoula, to the attention he showed her. How... devoted he'd seemed to the task of making love to her. Now that she thought about it, it did seem as if he'd been determined to make it last. Had she been the first woman he'd bedded in a while? The thought caused a shiver to race up her spine.

The wagon she'd been watching came to a stop, the man at the reins hopping to the ground before turning to help the woman and child down. He turned to face her and Laurel's breath caught. She blinked twice, widening her eyes to make sure she was seeing what she thought she was.

The man looked exactly like Holden.

She turned and found Holden near the creek, smiling at something the man in the first wagon said and she looked back and forth between the two men for long minutes before the woman she'd met at the festival, Abigail, joined her. Laurel opened her mouth to speak but nothing came out.

"They're twins." Abigail's light laughter caught on the breeze and Laurel exhaled the breath she'd been holding. "It's a bit shocking the first time you see them but it's easy to tell them apart once they're side by side." She grabbed Laurel's arm, turning her attention to where Holden and the other man stood. "That's Morgan, Holden's oldest brother and my husband." She turned them back to Holden's twin and the woman. "And that's Colton, but everyone calls him Colt. His wife is Sarah and that's their daughter, Emma. She's one and Sarah is expecting another come spring."

Laurel turned to face Abigail and wondered what Holden had told his family about her. Meeting Abigail at the festival and having her rescue her from Edna seemed a bit preplanned now that she thought about it. She narrowed her eyes and asked. "Holden's told you about me?"

Abigail looked surprised. "Nothing other than you're the new school teacher." She laughed suddenly. "The look on his face when he talked about you makes it obvious to us all that he liked you. Which is why we insisted he invite you to our picnic. I've never seen the man blush but he did today."

Her giggles were constant and Laurel wondered why Holden's reaction was so comical. She had an uneasy feeling, wondering if she was the butt of their jokes and mortification burned in her chest.

When Abigail turned to look at her, her smile vanished. "I've upset you. What did I say?"

"Nothing."

"I did, I can tell by the look on your face." Abigail turned to look back at the men where they were spreading blankets and placing the baskets she assumed contained the food. "I'm sorry. I didn't mean to make you uncomfortable. It's just that I've known

Holden for nearly two years and this is the first time I've ever seen him the slightest bit interested in a woman. According to his brothers, he's lived like a hermit since his wife Maggie died."

Laurel's face burned from embarrassment but hearing Abigail say she wasn't making fun of her caused the ache to subside. "That's what Alexandra told me, too, but I wasn't sure if she was correct or not."

Abigail smiled at her and looped her arm through Laurel's. "I'm sorry if I upset you but please, come join us. I know Sarah is dying to meet you and when Tristan and Emmaline get back from Idaho, they'll have questions we can't answer." She paused and grinned. "Tristan is Holden's baby brother and Emmaline is his wife. You'll get a chance to meet them soon, I'm sure."

"Are there any more family members I should know about?"

Abigail shook her head. "No. No one other than their father, James, but he doesn't talk much. Well, he talks to Sarah but we think that's because she favors their mother. There's just the four brothers and all their wives." She quirked an eyebrow up at Laurel. "And adding one more to the family wouldn't be frowned upon."

Laurel's heart kicked in her chest. "I'm sorry to disappoint you, but that isn't going to happen. Well, not with me."

"So sure already? But you don't even know Holden."

I know enough, Laurel thought, but kept the knowledge to herself.

Abigail escorted her to where the others had gathered and Laurel tried, and failed, to not look at Holden. Just seeing him there in the shade of the trees, with shafts of sunlight breaking through the branches caused her pulse to race. He was so handsome and the way he looked at her caused very unladylike notions to fill her head. If things weren't as they were, she'd happily let that man court her and hope for the best but the happily ever after she'd read about in dime novels wasn't in her future. She'd already tried and had failed miserably.

The men wandered off, leaving the women to set out all the food and when Sarah pulled a familiar looking pie plate from her basket, Laurel's heart skipped a beat.

"Do you want to know what Holden gave for your pie?"

Heat crawled up Laurel's neck and settled on her cheeks. "He bought my pie?"

"Just barely." Sarah laughed as she set it on the blanket. "For a minute there, I thought Joseph, the hotel owner, would win but Holden wasn't leaving without that pie. It fetched more money than any other dessert on the entire table!"

"Edna wasn't pleased by that bit of knowledge either," Abigail said, laughing.

Their laughter was mingled with good-natured ribbing and they talked quietly as they removed the food from the baskets. Laurel had a hard time keeping her attention on the conversation, and away from Holden, and was glad of the distraction the women's daughters made. Her heart broke when Elizabeth, Abigail's daughter had climbed into her lap and started babbling, telling her in her own special language about the doll she held. She smiled, listened to Elizabeth chatter and hoped her face didn't show her despair.

Looking up after long minutes of holding Elizabeth, she knew it did. The look on Holden's face told her so. She looked away and hoped the day would end quickly. The faster she got away from Holden and his family, the better off she'd be.

LAUREL HAD BEEN SITTING on the creek bank avoiding most everyone for the past hour and Holden wondered what she was thinking about so intently as he crossed the space to where she sat. She'd looked uncomfortable since coming to join the others, especially when she held Elizabeth. He wasn't sure why, though, and he wanted to know.

He stopped when he reached her, sat down and lifted his hat, combing a hand through his hair before laying the hat beside him. "You don't look as if you're enjoying yourself."

"And what gives you that impression?"

Holden smiled and picked up a blade of grass before tucking it between his lips. "If you want to go back to town, I'll take you. There's no reason for you to be miserable."

"I'm not miserable." She sighed, her shoulders slumping before she turned her head to look at him. "I'm sorry. I've not been very good company."

He shrugged one shoulder. "I didn't expect you to even come so I can't complain. Just having you here is enough."

She sighed again and he turned to look at her. Her hair was falling around her face and he lifted his hand, pushing the strands back behind her ear. "Why are you being so ornery towards me? Towards everyone in town?"

"What makes you think I'm not always like this?"

He grinned. "Because despite you not wanting to admit it, I spent nearly twelve hours with you and I know better."

"Maybe me being nice was all an act."

Her face held no hint of amusement but her eyes did. Holden leaned back on one arm, straightened his legs, crossing them at the ankle and turned his body slightly toward her. "It wasn't an act. You're just too stubborn to admit that you actually like me."

She snorted, unladylike and shook her head. "You think too highly of yourself, Holden Avery. The truth is, I drank too much and let my lowered inhibitions get the better of me. Had I been sober, I would have never allowed you into my room."

When she glanced at him, he grinned. "I recall you inviting me to your room then promised me things no 'lady' would dare mention once I got there." Her cheeks turned a becoming shade of pink and when she tried to look away, he reached out and took hold of her chin. "I'm not asking for much, Laurel, just a chance to get to know you better. That's all."

"I distinctly remember you mentioning marriage."

His smile widened. Marriage was what he wanted. "What's so wrong with that?"

"I could name half a dozen things but I'll spare you. I can't give you what you want, Holden. I can be your friend if you wish but that's all."

Disappointment settled like a rock in his gut. "Why?"

She opened her mouth as if to answer but shut it and turned her head.

"Laurel…"

"I don't need a man in my life nor do I want one. Ever." She turned back to face him, her eyes taking on a slight glassy look. "I'm sorry, Holden, but I can't give you anything other than what you already have."

She stood and left him sitting there under the shade trees with more questions than he had answers. His thoughts of courting her all proper like, shriveled in an instant. He blew out a frustrated breath, bent one leg and propped his arm on his knee, and stared at the water trickling by. Something wasn't right where Laurel was concerned and her refusal to be civil to people made that more apparent.

The distant sound of thunder made him look up. Clouds were rolling in over the mountain and the promise of rain was hard to ignore. He'd had plans to woo Laurel under a Montana sky but it looked as if nature itself was conspiring against him. Maybe it was a sign. Laurel apparently didn't want anything to do with him so why did he even bother trying?

He turned to look over at her where she sat with Abigail and Sarah. His pulse leaped again when she turned those smoky eyes on him and he knew. He wanted her more now than he did the night he first met her and he wouldn't stop trying to win her over. Even if the approaching storm called off the dance, and put an end to all his plans, he'd find a way to get through to her. He'd waited too long to find her to let her go now.

CHAPTER 6

"Where are you going all gussied up?"

Holden grinned at Alex and dusted off his hat before placing it on his head. "Going into town."

She gave him a long look from head to toe before her eyes widened. "You ain't going to see those ladies in the saloon are ya?" She crossed her arms over her chest and lifted her chin. "You promised me you wouldn't ever go see those hussies, pa, and I expect you to do as you say."

Holden laughed and leaned down to place a kiss on top of her head. "I'm not going to the saloon and remind me to tell your Aunt Sarah not every woman in the saloon is of ill repute."

She snorted. "Aunt Sarah says they jump on men the minute they walk in the door. That's why Uncle Colt ain't allowed in there anymore."

"Is that so?"

"Yep. Aunt Sarah says no decent man should be in there courting those type of women."

"Well, you've nothing to worry about. I have no intentions of courting those women." He left his room and headed for the stairs, Alex hot on his heels.

"Why you going into town all dressed up then?" She gasped suddenly, her eyes widening again and a horrified look crossed her face. "Pa, don't you dare go see her!"

He couldn't help but laugh. "See who?"

"That devil woman." She ran to him, grabbed his arm, and made him stop walking. "She don't like you, remember? She don't like anyone and going to talk to her will just make you cranky like it always does. Stay home with me. We can saddle my pony and your black and go for a ride."

Holden smiled, peering down at her before stooping to be eye level with her. "That sounds like a fine idea." Her pleased smile nearly did him in. "But not today."

She frowned then crossed her arms over her chest again. Her defiant attitude was cute when she was six. Now, it only spelled trouble for the future. As much as he hated to admit it, Laurel was right where his daughter was concerned. He couldn't let her continue to act the way she did and knowing what he was about to do, Alex was going to be a handful for weeks to come.

He took a deep breath, smiling to lessen the blow. "I like her, Alex. I'm just going to ask her to supper."

She tried to interrupt but he held up his hand, stopping her. "In the hotel restaurant. I know I'd be asking too much to bring her back here so for now, I'll go to town when I want to see her."

That horrified look on her face grew. "You mean this ain't no one time thing?"

He shook his head.

Her shoulders dropped, her arms fell away from her chest and she looked as if he'd killed every one of her beloved critters. "You're going to court her, ain't ya, pa?"

"If she'll let me." He grinned. "And probably even if she don't."

Alex huffed out a breath and turned, walking down the stairs, her steps heavy and forlorn. He watched her cross to the front door and leave the house without another word. He sighed and followed her.

She was sitting on the steps when he walked outside, her head hung. Holden sat down beside her and waited.

It took her close to ten minutes before she looked up. Her eyes were glassy and he knew she was fighting tears.

"I don't want no new momma."

"I know you don't." He smiled and wrapped his arm around her shoulders, pulling her closer to his side. "If I had my way, your momma would have never left us. She'd be in the house, fluttering around the kitchen and making a fuss about something she'd burned." Kissing the top of her head, he gave her a small squeeze. "But, we can't change the past, Alex. We just have to move on and live our life to the best of our ability."

"You gonna ask Miss Montgomery to marry you?"

He already had, in a round about way, but didn't dare tell Alex. He smiled and stood up. "Let's not get ahead of ourselves. I'm just going to ask her to supper. Talk to her a little bit." He turned to look at her. "If you're lucky, I'll realize I don't actually like her all that much and that she turns into some foul creature when the moon is full."

Alex brightened and stood. "She probably does. Some horrid beast with two heads."

"Let's hope not. Hard to tell what she'd do to me if that was the case."

He left her standing on the porch, worry etching her face in troubled lines. He knew the moment he decided to head into town Alex would take issue with it but he'd lived the better part of ten years doing nothing but seeing that she had the best of everything he could give her. He'd stayed home, tending to her while his brothers headed to town every weekend to visit those ladies in the saloon and not once had he regretted it. He'd do whatever it took to make Alex happy but he couldn't give on this one thing.

Truth was, he'd watched so many people happily go about their lives and envied most of them. He envied his brothers, all married now and planning their futures, making room for babies, and a part of him died every time he saw how happy they were. He wanted that too. He wanted it for Alex. He wanted to see her smile. To become the kind of woman her mother would be proud of and he couldn't do that alone. He needed help and the woman who could help him do that was an ornery piece of work but she stirred his blood and made his long neglected body ache in ways he couldn't ignore anymore.

He wanted her. Plain and simple. Waspish tongue and displeasing disposition that Laurel Montgomery had, he wanted her. And he aimed to have her whether she liked it or not.

LAUREL HAD JUST ROUNDED the schoolhouse when she saw him and tried to duck back around the building. He smiled at her and she sighed. He'd seen her.

She took a moment to compose herself, inhaled a few steadying breaths and wondered how she'd be able to lash out at the man again. It killed her every time she did.

Two full months in town and everywhere she looked, there he was. She nearly sighed just thinking of him. He was everything she'd ever thought she wanted in a man. Someone strong and handsome. A hard worker with a gentle smile and a pleasing tone of voice that didn't make her insides shake at the mere sound of it.

He was also persistent and borderline irritating. And she couldn't help the nervous butterflies that were awakened at the mere sight of him.

She rounded the corner and walked to the sidewalk, trying to think of something to say to him but he beat her to it, giving her one of those little smiles she liked so much and tipping his hat at her. "Mind if I walk with you?"

"Will you go away if I say I'd rather be alone?"

"Probably not."

"Somehow, I didn't think so." He fell into step with her and Laurel clutched her reticule, pulling her coat tighter against her, and tried not to notice how tall he was, or how wonderful he smelled. Like fresh hay and sun dried clothes. "I'm just going to the end of the street, Holden. I'm sure I can make it there just fine on my own."

He looked down at her and smiled again. "I'm sure you can but seeing how that's where I'm headed, it seems a bit silly to walk on the other side of the road."

Laurel glanced up at him and wished she hadn't. He was far too handsome for her good sense, especially when he looked at her as if he was thinking things a decent man wouldn't dare to think about a woman he barely knew. Those butterflies were back and her pulse fluttered.

They reached the end of town, the hotel with its newly painted exterior looking as spiffy as any she'd seen. The diners filling the restaurant were clearly seen through the window and even though she was near starving, walking inside that building was getting harder every day.

Holden walked to the door, opened it and held it for her. She stared at him, wondering why he still went out of his way to be nice to her after she'd plainly told him she wasn't interested in anything more from him. "Why are you here?"

He had the decency to blush before letting the door swing back shut. "Well, to be honest, Laurel, I'm here for you. I plan on courting you all proper like whether you like it or not."

It was her turn to blush now. She swallowed to moisten her throat and blinked at him. "Why? I've already told you my feelings about it."

That grin was back. He tipped the front of his hat up with one finger, meeting her gaze head on. "Truth is, despite your surly attitude and your rude behavior towards everyone in town, me especially, I just can't stop thinking about you. You can fight me until you're blue in the face, Laurel, but I'm not going anywhere. I'll dog your every step until you see I'm the man you're supposed to be with. We belong together."

Her face burned at his admission and her heart was beating so hard she wondered if he could hear it. She looked down the street, noticing the people still milling about town on a Friday evening and wondered if her playing it safe, and keeping her distance from everyone, was what was making life so miserable. She hadn't always felt this way. In the dozen or so towns she'd found herself in since leaving home, she'd been happy. Now, happiness seemed an illusive creature and the man standing in front of her was the reason.

Turning her attention back to Holden, she released a pent up breath and met his gaze. He was still watching her, the look on his face saying he wasn't going anywhere, and if she were honest with herself, she'd know she didn't want him to.

She shook her head at him and smiled. "Fine. Since it's obvious you're not going to go away, I'll make a deal with you. Stop asking me for things I'm not ever going to give you, and stop getting on my nerves, and I might let you escort me to supper on occasion."

The smile he graced her with would have lit a starless night. Her insides quivered as she looked at him and when he crossed the space between them and took her hand, her heart skipped a beat.

"All I'm asking for is a chance, Laurel." He lifted her hand, kissed her palm so softly she barely felt the contact before letting her go and reaching for the door to the hotel.

He held it open for her as she walked inside and when everyone saw her, their frowns grew when Holden laid a hand on the small of her back and led her into the dining room. The whispers started immediately and Laurel kept her chin raised, ignoring those staring and her knees were wobbly by the time they'd reached an empty table.

Holden was a perfect gentleman, holding her chair for her, waiting until she was settled before removing his hat and sitting down. The waitress wasted no time coming to the table and the look of shock and curiosity on her face wasn't missed.

They were quiet as they looked over the evening menu and once they'd ordered, the waitress leaving them alone, Laurel was at a loss of what to say.

She reached for her water glass, noticed her hand was shaking and inhaled a deep, steadying breath.

"I didn't realize having supper with me would make you so uncomfortable."

Looking up, Laurel saw the concern on his face. "I'd be uncomfortable if I were sitting alone. You've not changed the fact that no one here likes me."

"You've not made it easy for anyone to like you."

She hid a smile behind her glass. "True."

The food arrived in record time and Laurel knew the company she kept was the reason why. She wasn't going to complain, not when the food on her plate was still steaming and smelled so delicious she hoped her stomach didn't rumble from the mere sight of it.

They ate in silence for long minutes before Holden looked up at her. "So, rumor has it you're from Arizona but I know for a fact you call Seattle home."

Laurel dropped her fork, the noise alerting several other patrons who looked over at her. She looked up, horrified and stammered like an idiot before closing her mouth with a snap.

"Don't worry. Your secret is safe with me."

He knew where she was really from? How did he know? She narrowed her eyes at him, anger and indignation coloring her face. "That brother of yours, the marshal, he's been snooping, hasn't he?"

Holden leaned forward, his voice a soft whisper when he said,

"Snooping enough to know you never stay in any one place for very long."

She blanched and leaned back in her seat. "What else do you know?"

He smiled and went back to eating. "Not much.

Laurel felt ill. The food on her plate looked less appetizing by the second and she found it hard to breathe all of a sudden.

"Hey, take a deep breath, Laurel."

He took her hand, gave it a light squeeze, and Laurel looked up. Concern clouded his eyes.

The many places she'd tried to rebuild her life in flashed before her eyes and each one left behind such guilt and remorse, she was nearly overwhelmed. Her eyes misted and she blinked to chase the tears away. Holden's hand, still warm and comforting against her own, eased some of the pain. "Don't tell anyone, Holden."

"Why?"

She looked down at her plate. "I can't tell you."

He didn't respond and Laurel was glad for it. She wasn't ready for anyone to know of her past, especially him. She tugged her hand free from his, retrieved her dropped fork from the table and smiled. "So, tell me, Holden, did you sneak away from your ranch or did you have to leave, dragging Alexandra along behind you when she found out you were coming to see me?"

His laughter lifted her mood and it wasn't until their meal was completed that she realized how free she felt. She hadn't laughed in so long, she'd almost forgotten how wonderful it felt.

They shared a dessert, a slice of apple pie he said wasn't nearly as good as the one she'd baked and Laurel blushed to her roots when he told her how much he'd had to pay for it at the auction.

The stars dotted a clear sky as they left the hotel restaurant and the air had a bite to it. She tugged her coat closer as they walked back to the school. They both seemed to be lost in thought and the trip was made in silence. When they reached her door at the back of the school, Laurel was almost afraid to tell him goodnight.

She'd been courted a few times in her life and almost every one of those men had certain expectations at the end of the evening. Those expectations caused the butterflies she'd been fighting to control all night to swim so dizzyingly she had to take a few deep breaths to calm them down.

Holden was staring at her when she finally got the nerve to turn and look at him. Her pulse started racing the moment she did. Those expectations most men thought were their due weren't so bewildering as she looked at Holden. If truth be known, she'd say the nervousness she felt was from the fact he wasn't formally courting her and wouldn't expect any sort of goodnight kiss. She blushed when she realized she wanted it, despite what she'd told him earlier.

"Well." She tried to get her heated cheeks to cool but failed miserably when her gaze drifted to his mouth. Lord he had such nice lips. They were soft, too, she remembered and of all the men she'd ever kissed in her life, none had done it so expertly as Holden did. "Thank you for a lovely evening." He smiled at her, shifted his weight to one foot and Laurel felt dizzy all of a sudden. The anxiety was killing her. "Goodnight!"

She whirled on her heel, rushed inside her room and slammed the door, her heart beating so hard against her ribcage she felt foolish. She was a grown woman, not some simpering school girl but she felt like one. Giddy. Breathless. Hopeless.

Falling in love with a man she barely knew.

Sighing, she leaned back against the door, her arms falling to her sides. "You are an idiot, Laurel."

Turning her head toward the window, she wondered if she could see him from there but didn't dare move. If he saw her staring out at him, she'd die of mortification.

HOLDEN WAS HALFWAY DOWN the street before he stopped, turned around, and walked back to the school house.

Since the moment Laurel had slammed her door in his face, he'd gone over everything Morgan had learned about her, and told him about, and every piece of information he was able to get from Laurel himself and none of it explained why she was so stand-offish at times.

Or why he got the impression her surly attitude was all an act.

She confused him more often than not and tonight was no exception. It had been a long time since he'd courted a woman and from what he remembered, there were certain things one hoped he got at the end of the evening. A kiss goodnight being one of them. A kiss he'd been anticipating until Laurel shouted goodnight to him and slammed the door in his face.

He'd seen her gaze linger on his mouth as they reached the room behind the school house and that was all it took for his cock to take notice and jump alive as if a hot coal had been shoved into his pants. He hadn't made his intentions of courting her be known yet, but by the time he left town tonight, Laurel would know it.

Rounding the school house, he didn't stop until he was on the little stoop by her door. He knocked, the sound loud in the surrounding stillness and when Laurel opened the door, her shocked gaze landing on him, he was near shaking with the need to have her.

She'd let her hair down, all those glorious curls dangling down her back and framing her face so perfectly, and he almost forgot why he'd turned back around and banged on her door as he stared at her.

"Holden? Did you forget something?"

He forgot something all right. His manners. "Yes, ma'am. I do believe I did." He reached for her, weaving his fingers into her hair and pulling her toward him, kissing her without another word, her shocked gasp giving him the entrance into her mouth within seconds. Her hands clutched his shirt and it only took a few seconds to realize she wasn't fighting him like he thought she might, but was clinging to him, her tongue tangling with his own, little mewling noises escaping her throat and making the incessant throbbing in his groin more profound.

She pulled away after long moments, panting for breath, and those amber eyes he'd admired the first time he saw her were shining with something he hadn't seen directed at him since the night he'd spent with her in Missoula.

Lust. Desire.

Her arms were around his neck in the next instant, her mouth so hot and wet against his own. Holden wrapped her in his arms, pulled her into his body and took everything he wanted from that kiss. Deepened it until he had trouble breathing past his need for her.

She took a step backwards and pulled him into her room, the door kicked shut without ever breaking contact with his mouth.

He turned her, braced her back against the door, his fingers moving into those luscious locks of hair and he was hard and aching by the time she pulled back for air. Her eyes glistened. Her lips wet and swollen and it took everything in him not to guide her to the bed and have his way with her.

Laurel inhaled a few deep breaths and blinked lazily at him. "I didn't want anyone to see us on the stoop." Her hands slid away from his shoulders to rest on his chest. "If anyone caught you in here, I would lose my job."

"I won't let that happen." She blinked up lazily at him, licked her lips and sent his thoughts racing in directions they shouldn't have. "I didn't come back to invite myself to your bed so your position as school teacher is safe."

She nodded, her gaze lowering to his chest briefly. "And why did you come back?"

He grinned and put a finger under her chin, lifting her head so he could see her. "Because I wanted a kiss. I thought that was obvious." Even though the room was bathed in shadows, he could see her cheeks redden.

"Is that all you wanted?"

He laughed. "Not by a long shot, darlin', but I'm a patient man. I can wait."

She smiled up at him, lifted up on her toes and kissed him again, this time without the frenzy of hurried motions. It was soft, lingering and he cursed his neglected groin for demanding so much attention and distracting him. When she broke the kiss, her lips swollen from his kiss, he knew being a gentleman would be harder than he thought it would. Especially when she whispered, "Make love to me."

○

COMMON SENSE TOLD her to let him leave but she'd made many stupid decisions in her life, what was one more? He was still staring down at her, his breathing as labored as hers. She raised her hands, her fingers brushing the buttons on the front of his shirt and the need to touch him, skin to skin was too much.

She popped the first button, glancing up at his face as she unhooked the others. "Don't read more into this than there is, Holden."

He watched her hands, his chest rising quickly as she reached the last button on his shirt. "And what is this?"

Laurel nearly sighed when she pulled his shirt apart, his chest displayed in the filtered light coming from the single lamp on the table. She looked up into his eyes and licked her lips. "I want you."

His nostrils flared, his hands resting on her waist, tightening.

"I'm not making any promises about the future. Call me selfish but all I want is for you to make love to me like you did in Missoula. Make me feel something other than misery."

He stared at her for long minutes, the thoughts crossing his mind shining in his eyes before he nodded his head at her. "One day at a time, Laurel." He pulled his shirt from his pants, tossing it to the floor.

Much like their one night in Missoula, they undressed each other amid breathless kisses, their clothes thrown across the room to land in a growing pile on the floor. The air inside her room was cool but she ignored it, the warmth of his body more than enough to keep her from shivering.

He kissed her again while cupping her bottom in his hands, lifting her slightly until she felt him against her slick folds. She broke the kiss, stared at him as he slid inside of her, and her sharp inhale of breath filled the silence in the room.

Bracing her back against the door, he grabbed her left leg, wrapped it around his waist and never took his eyes off of her as he slid in and out of her, the heat from his body burning when they made contact.

He watched her, intense concentration on his face as he loved her and it wasn't until her stomach clenched that she realized how different this time was from their night in Missoula. Then, it had been all about the pleasure of it. Rough, mindless abandon with one goal in mind. Now, it was felt soul deep. She could see it in his eyes, feel it burn in her own, and her heart ached to the point she couldn't breathe.

Wrapping his arms around her, he picked her up, turned and walked to her small bed, laying her down before kissing her. Their limbs entwined, sweat soaked skin slid against the other and when he lifted his head to look at her and whispered, "marry me," she grinned, wrapped both legs around his waist and said, "no."

His thrusts became harder while his soft whispers of "marry me" were a constant echo in her ear.

When she climaxed, her nails were digging into his back, her hips lifting to meet his thrusts, she bit her tongue to keep from screaming out, "yes" to his adamant demand.

He stopped long enough to let her catch her breath before he started moving again, the intense look on his face still there but something in his eyes promised things that made her stomach quiver. His thrusts became harder, his head lowering to capture one nipple between his lips and as he suckled her, his cock filling her so completely, Laurel knew she'd never be able to stick to her plan. Not with him. She wanted him too much. Her body craved him to the point of desperation. Ached to have him, always, and she knew... consequences be damned, she'd let him have his way and have her. She just hoped her heart would survive it.

CHAPTER 7

A ROOSTER CROWED SOMEWHERE in town and Laurel blinked against the inky darkness of her room. Holden stirred behind her, his arm tightening around her waist, his lips tickling a path across the back of her neck. She smiled and pulled the blankets up, tucking them under her chin.

They lay quietly for long minutes, neither speaking, fingers seeking out warm places on each other's skin until Holden sighed, kissed her shoulder and crawled from the bed.

Laurel watched him dress, admired the play of muscle under his skin and wondered if she was doing the right thing. In the heat of the moment, the mind could be fooled enough to accept almost anything but once the sun rose, would letting this man love her seem as wonderful as it had the night before?

Old fears resurfaced, the play of memories that tormented her most days whispered for her to protect her heart. To not trust him but when he turned to look at her and smiled, she willed her heart to silence.

It had been so long since a man looked at her like that. Looked at her as if he saw nothing but her and the feeling was euphoric. She returned his smile and sat up, tucking her knees into her chest while securing the blankets around her. "Can you make it back to the ranch without anyone knowing you were out all night?"

He chuckled and shook his head. "Not likely. The ranch hands will see me come in but Alex should still be in the bed." He picked up his discarded hat from the ground and dusted off the brim. "She's the only one I care about knowing. The rest don't matter."

He crossed the room, his booted feet hitting the floor loud enough to echo in the silence. Sitting on the side of the bed, he pushed her hair over one shoulder and leaned down, laying a kiss to the skin he'd exposed. "Thank you for last night."

Laurel blushed, glad the room was bathed in shadows. "Don't thank me. It makes it seem sordid if you do."

"All right." He stared at her for several long moments before grinning. "Can I come calling on you again?"

It was Laurel's turn to laugh. "I'll feel completely used if you don't."

"Does that mean I can court you openly, then?"

The moment of truth. Did she want him to court her? Men didn't court women for lack of better things to do. They did it in an attempt to woo them into marriage and Holden had already told her that's what he wanted. Did she?

Memories of the past night replayed through her head and the pleasant shivers of anticipation running laps up and down her spine were answer enough. She leaned forward, kissed him softly on the lips and smiled when she pulled away. "Don't do anything crazy. I've had enough attention as it is. Having you come running to town everyday with bushels of flowers will be embarrassing."

Wrapping her in a hug, he kissed her until her toes tingled, her stomach clenched and desire burned hot and needy through her body.

"I'll try not to embarrass you," he said. "But be warned, I've not courted a woman since before I married Maggie. I'm prone to overdo it on occasion."

They talked until the sky started to lighten with streaks of pink and orange then she wrapped herself in the bed sheets and walked him to the door. More kisses and soft whispers filled the air and when he asked to escort her to the dance the following weekend, she didn't dread the prospect of going. She had something to look forward to now.

Letting go of the past was harder said than done but it was time to come out into the open and shine as she once did. And with the man now sneaking around the side of the school house, she knew that was once again possible.

⌣

THE SUN WAS PEEKING over the mountain when Holden drew to a stop by the barn. Pete, one of the ranch hands, gave him a knowing smile as he walked over and took the reins of his horse from him before leading the animal into the barn.

The house was quiet but wood smoke could be seen from the chimney in the back. Issac was up and preparing breakfast, as usual.

Holden took the front steps two at a time, the smile on his face, he knew, would be there for days. He wasn't sure what he'd done to finally break through Laurel's reservations about him but he couldn't be happier. He'd have done just about anything to win her over but it didn't look as if he'd have much trouble now. All he had to do now was convince Alex that she wasn't a she-devil like she supposed she was.

Entering the house and walking to the stairs, he started up but froze on the third step. Alex was sitting on the second floor landing, a hard scowl painted on her otherwise cherubic face. Her eyes were narrowed, her mouth pinched into a thin white line and he blew out a breath.

He climbed the remaining steps and sat on the top one, leaning his back against the wall. He didn't say a word, just looked over at her and waited.

When she stared back, the disgruntled look on her face becoming more fierce, dread filled him. Of all the things he wanted in life, Alex's happiness was foremost in his mind. If she didn't accept Laurel... He didn't even want to think about it. He couldn't choose between them. Alex would win every time.

She said nothing for long minutes, the ticking of a clock somewhere in the house the only noise and the longer she sat staring at him, the angrier he became. He knew she was upset, and really couldn't blame her. It had just been the two of them for so long, the change was sure to be upsetting, but he needed to remember who the adult was.

Shifting his position, he gave her a stern look and said, "Say it. Whatever it is. Let's have this out once and for all."

She exploded. He barely understood a word she said her words erupted in such violent succession that she was winded in a matter of moments. He let her vent, watched her face turn bright red and when tears filled her eyes, sliding down her cheeks to splash on her nightgown, he sighed, rubbed a hand over his face and reached for her.

He hadn't heard her cry so hard in ages, the last time being two years ago when she fell from a tree in the backyard and bruised her ribs. He let her cry until she was hiccupping so badly, he thought she'd lose her breath completely.

Sitting her up, he wiped her tears away, placed a kiss on her forehead and pulled her back against him. They sat in silence until he heard his father stirring in his room, until the smell of bacon and oven-fresh biscuits filled the house. Leaning back to look at her face, he smiled, pushed her hair away from her damp cheeks and said, "I love you, you know."

Alex sniffled and scrubbed a fist across her nose. "I know."

"I only want you to be happy, Alex. That's all I've ever wanted for you."

"I know."

He bit his tongue for a moment, wondering exactly how to say what he wanted to. She looked up, her large, luminous eyes still glassy with unshed tears. "You stayed all night with her, didn't you?"

Holden's face heated and he knew he was blushing. Having your ten-year-old daughter know you'd been sleeping with a woman was about the most embarrassing thing he'd ever have to live through—he hoped. He cleared his throat and avoided her gaze. "I want her to be my wife, Alex." She opened her mouth, to protest, he was sure, but he silenced her with a raised hand. "Let me finish, all right?"

She sighed and nodded.

"I love you, Alex, you know I do, and as much as I enjoy taking care of you and this ranch, I need more." She glanced up at him and it was all he could do to keep looking at her. "I get lonely, Alex. Every man does at some point in his life."

"Why? I'm here. Grandpa Avery is here. Aren't we enough?"

He grinned. Talk like this he hadn't thought would come at such an early age but with Alex, he'd stopped trying to predict her long ago. She was wise beyond her years, most days, and today was one of those days.

"Thing is, Alex, a man wants certain things out of life. He wants a home, a family and having someone there to share all that with him just makes it all the better." He glanced down at her, kissing her forehead again. "I have you and grandpa but most days, it just isn't enough. I want more. I want someone I can talk to about anything. Someone to take care of me every once in a while and… and I want that person to be Laurel. I want a wife, Alex, but I can't choose between the two of you."

Her eyes brightened a bit before she sat up. "Then you mean if I say no, you'll stop going to see her?"

His heart ached at her words but he nodded his head. "If that's what you want, then yes. I'll stop seeing her."

The smile she graced him with brightened her whole face. She laughed and threw her arms around his neck, giving his stubbled cheek hard, smacking kisses before she let go, jumped to her feet and danced a jig, right there on the second floor landing. She ran all the way back to her room, her little girl giggles filling the house while the ache inside his chest constricted until he couldn't breathe past it.

He sat there staring at the banister, thoughts of Laurel playing in his mind relentlessly before he pushed the images away. Alex would never like her, regardless of what he said or did and her refusal to even try told him he'd failed in raising her right. She shouldn't be so close-minded but she was an Avery. If he knew anything, he knew they were a stubborn lot. Always had been and Alex proved they always would be.

And his future with Laurel was over before it even got started.

◡

Teaching, most days, was as pleasant an experience as Laurel always thought it would be but today was different. The children were rowdy, more so than usual, but for once, it wasn't Alexandra causing the uproar. She'd been unusually quiet most of the day, keeping her head down but every once in a while, Laurel would see her peeking up at her.

A nervous flutter caused her stomach to tremble every time she saw that look. It meant she knew things between her father and her school teacher had taken a turn and if Laurel had to guess, she'd say the girl wasn't happy and had their positions been reversed, she would have been in the exact same foul mood. Alexandra had asked her right out if she wanted to court her father and Laurel had said no. Now, not even two weeks later, that had all changed.

She'd barely spoken to Holden when he dropped Alexandra off that morning. He'd looked rather subdued and she just assumed he didn't want to talk about what had transpired between them in public. With children clamoring to get inside the building and people walking the street outside the school, stolen kisses weren't an option either so she'd dismissed the whole thing as him just being discreet.

But now, as the children got more wild with every passing minute, and Alexandra still gave her those silent, death-stares, she had to wonder. Had Holden not spoken more than a few words to her for a reason? And was that reason sitting in front of her now, watching her like a hawk circling her prey?

The uneasy feeling didn't go away. It grew worse when she dismissed class and Alexandra lingered behind, taking her time gathering her things. Laurel was on the front stoop, wishing the children a good day but kept glancing over her shoulder at Alexandra. Something wasn't right. Alexandra was usually the first one out the door at the end of the day, seeing her lag behind meant something was wrong.

Glancing at the road, and not seeing Holden on his black stallion coming her way, Laurel turned and walked back into the classroom. She gave Alexandra a glance as she walked to her desk. She busied herself sorting the books and slates left piled on one corner while casting small glances up at the girl.

Five minutes later, Alexandra was still there, standing by her desk, staring at her. Dread filled like venom in Laurel's stomach. She sat the books in her hand aside, cleared off the corner of her desk and perched on the edge of the desk, folding her hands into her lap. "Is there something you'd like to talk about?"

Alexandra blew out a bored breath. "No. Would you like to talk about anything?"

Laurel opened her mouth but shut it with a snap. Was this girl really only ten years old? She wasn't overly tall but looked her age for the most part, until you looked into her eyes. The intelligence

Laurel saw there most of the time was astounding. Today was no different. A little girl in boys trousers and a chambray shirt, her pigtails lying across her shoulders, she looked every bit as mature as most teen girls. Holden would have his hands full very soon. She was positive.

"Will your father be late in picking you up?"

Alexandra shrugged one shoulder in reply.

"All right," Laurel said. She stared at the girl until the uneasiness grew and sent cold chills down her spine. "What is it, Alexandra? If you have something to say, then just say it."

"Fine. I don't like you much."

Laurel smiled. "That's obvious."

"I don't want you for my momma, either."

A nod of her head was all Laurel could give her in response. Alexandra crossed the room and stopped in front of the desk, her big blue eyes shining up at her. "My grandpa said I was being selfish."

"I thought your grandpa didn't talk?"

Alexandra shrugged. "He talks to me all the time." She shifted her weight to one foot and sighed. "He said I can't tell pa who to marry and me saying he can't marry you is wrong. That I have to be happy for him no matter how much I don't like ya. He said that my pa's let his life pass him by so he could take care of me and it's wrong to not let him have something that would make him happy."

She looked away, sighed again and shook her head in defeat. "I'll probably never like ya but my pa does so I'll just have to be okay with it." She looked up, raised a hand to scratch at her cheek and lowered her hand to the desk. "Pa always takes me to eat supper in the hotel on Monday. I guess it would be okay if you wanted to come along. Heaven knows he'll just be wishing you was there anyway."

Laurel held back the beaming smile trying to form and was able to keep it restrained as she nodded her head at her. "That's very nice of you, Alexandra, but if supper in the hotel is your special time with your father, then I'll not intrude."

Alexandra shrugged her shoulder and turned. "Suit yourself." She gathered her things, clasping them in her arms before turning back to face her. "Just let him know I offered, all right?"

"I'll do that."

Laurel watched her walk away and exit the building, pulling the door shut behind her, her invitation to dine with them still playing through her head like a soft musical note. She grinned and stood, walking to the window at the front of the room, peering outside. Alexandra was by the gate, Holden coming down the road on his black stallion, and when he reached the girl, he scooped her from the ground with one arm and headed to the hotel without stopping. Just as they were about to ride out of sight, Holden turned his head, peering over his shoulder. He smiled back at her and Laurel lifted her hand, waving as they rode away.

Alexandra's words whispered themselves to her on repeat as she cleaned the classroom, putting away the lesson books and straightening the desks. The smile on her face, she knew, would be permanent. Alexandra still didn't like her but the girl wasn't going to fight her father in his attempts to court her. As much as she'd like to have joined them for supper, she knew it was too soon. Alexandra would need time to ease into the situation and after so long a time running from her past, Laurel would too.

She was turning toward the door leading to her little room in the back of the school when the front door opened. Turning to find Holden there surprised her more than Alexandra's admission that she would be all right with her father courting her. He smiled, crossed the room and wrapped his arms around her, kissing her breathless before she could even get a word out. When he lifted his head to look at her, his eyes were dancing with laughter. "So I hear you refused Alex's supper invitation?"

Laurel grinned. "I don't think she really wanted me there so I declined."

"Well, she probably wasn't sincere when the offer was made but she's mad as a wet hen now." He chuckled and stole another quick kiss. "To her way of thinking, you weren't refusing her, you were rejecting me and for some reason, even though she claims not to like you, she'll not let you just toss me away. Now go grab your things and come have supper with us."

They walked side by side all the way to the hotel and entering the building was nerve wracking. Alexandra was sitting at a table in the back of the room, toying with her napkin and looking as bored as she ever had. When she looked up and saw them, the corner of her mouth quirked into a half-smile.

"I knew you'd come if pa asked."

Laurel thanked Holden as he held the chair beside Alexandra and waited for her to settle before sitting across from them both. "Well, I can't say it was for him I came. Truth is, I really did want to have supper with you but I wasn't sure you really wanted me here, so I declined."

"Oh, well, from now on, take my first offer. I'll not be giving you any more second chances."

Her heart hadn't felt so light in ages. Laurel smiled and said, "Yes, ma'am," assuring Alexandra things wouldn't be so difficult in the future.

Supper passed with surprising ease, the banter at the table filled with laughter and as Holden and Alexandra escorted her back to the school, Laurel couldn't remember a time when she'd been so happy.

"I'll see you tomorrow," Holden said, as he left Alexandra by the horse and walked Laurel to the front door of the school.

"Tomorrow." She smiled when he glanced at her lips. Not being able to steal a kiss was probably as irritating to him as it was her but there would be plenty of time for that. The rest of her life if Holden has his way and for once, Laurel wasn't afraid of her future.

CHAPTER 8

THE WEEK PASSED in a blur and by the time the weekend rolled around, Laurel was fit to be tied. Holden had been true to his word and not done anything embarrassing in his attempt to court her but the things he said to her every day when he picked Alexandra up from school left her skin flushed, her stomach clenching in anticipation and need so profound to wash over her body she could barely contain it.

She tucked a few strands of loose hair back into the up-twist she'd pulled her hair into and looked at herself in the mirror one last time. Holden would be there any minute to escort her to the dance and she wondered what the night would bring. Inviting him into her bed again was a given but with Alexandra knowing they were officially a couple, he may opt to go home instead. She was still too impressionable to blatantly flaunt their doings in front of her and Laurel would bet money the girl would be watching the clock until her father returned.

The knock on her door startled her and she gave herself one last look before turning to answer it. Holden was leering at her when she pulled the door open and wasted no time walking inside the room, elbowing the door shut and mussing her hair as he leaned down to kiss her.

"God, I've missed you," he whispered between nips at her lips. "I didn't think today would ever get here."

Laurel moaned when he slid his tongue into her mouth, her bones felt liquid at the feel of his arms around her. He kissed a path to her ear, down the length of her neck and ended at the bodice of her dress, his lips leaving a wet trail over the top of her breasts.

"What say we skip the dance and get straight to the loving?"

Laurel giggled and shook her head. "Absolutely not. I've already had numerous people ask if I would be there and I've told them yes. If they discover us both not in attendance, my reputation will be in tatters."

He sighed and lifted his head, nibbling at her lips before laying his forehead against her own. "Fine. I'll take you to the dance, make sure everyone we know sees us both and then we'll sneak off."

"Now that, Mr. Avery, sounds like a very good idea."

He grabbed her shawl and draped it over her shoulders, his hand lingering on the brown sateen dress she'd been wearing the night they met. He gave her a knowing smile and opened the door for her, closing it behind them.

The street was filled with people, their laughter and voices carrying across town. Music could be heard filtering between the buildings and although the occasional gusty wind lent a bite to the air, Laurel had never felt so warm. Everything seemed perfect.

They stepped onto the sidewalk to avoid the stagecoach and cut between the mercantile and the telegraph office, emerging into the clearing behind it where everyone was congregating.

A makeshift dance floor had been erected and tables filled with refreshments laid out on top of colorful tablecloths. Lanterns hung from the trees, the soft glow from the candles casting the area in a soft, orange glow. Late summer flowers were tied in clusters to the tables, some gracing the chairs placed around the perimeter of the clearing and Laurel smiled when she took it all in. "For a town as small as Willow Creek, you certainly know how to throw a party."

Holden laughed and guided her across the clearing. Abigail and Morgan were near the refreshment table, talking in hushed tones but both of them smiled as they approached.

"I'm so glad you came," Abigail said, giving Laurel a warm hug. "I was afraid I'd be stuck with no female companionship for the evening. Edna would have insisted I spend the majority of my time talking with her had that been the case. For some odd reason, the woman likes to think of me as a schoolgirl with no direction in my life."

"Well, I'm glad to have helped. I've only known Edna a short time but I've seen how trying she can be on one's nerves."

They talked for long minutes amongst themselves until the musicians cranked up the volume of their instruments, strumming and picking the guitars louder to gain everyone's attention. The dance floor filled, happy couples twirling around the space and their happy laughter joined that of the music.

When Holden turned to her and smiled, Laurel offered her hand to his unspoken question. He led her to the dance floor, took her in his arms much too close for an unmarried couple and guided her into a lively dance step that had her laughing within minutes.

She couldn't remember a time when she'd been so happy. Holden's arms around her felt so—right. The scent of fresh hay and sun dried clothes that she'd come to associate with him was hypnotic and three dances later, she hoped the night would never end.

He escorted her back to the refreshment table where they both took a cup of some fruity tasting drink and headed back to the edge of the crowd where Morgan and Abigail were. They were both laughing and when Abigail turned to look at her, Laurel knew she and Holden were the topic of conversation. A sly glance to her right and a tilt of the head and Abigail left her husband's side and beckoned Laurel to follow. She excused herself and met Abigail a few steps away from the men.

"Talk the men can't hear?" Laurel asked when she stopped beside Abigail. "I'm almost afraid to ask."

Holden's sister-in-law laughed and cast a quick look toward the men. "Well, I wasn't sure if what I wanted to ask would be embarrassing or not so I thought the less ears that heard it, the more likely I'd get an honest answer."

Laurel's heart skipped a beat. What could Abigail possibly ask that would be embarrassing? She swallowed the lump forming in her throat and tried to smile. "Ask about what?"

Something in Abigail's eyes let Laurel know it wasn't anything terribly bad. Mirth shined behind those inquisitive eyes. "Well, last weekend, Morgan couldn't sleep and was out making his rounds in town before the sun rose." Abigail gave her a serious look, her eyes narrowed ever so much. "Seems he saw a suspicious looking character lurking around the school house and went to investigate."

"Oh?" Laurel bit her tongue. "Did he question the man?"

"No." Abigail's eyes widened. "Morgan said the man looked an awful lot like Holden but he couldn't for the life of him figure out why his brother would be sneaking around the school house in the predawn hours." Abigail glanced across the space that separated them from the men. "Would you know why he'd be there that early in the morning?"

Laurel could tell by the look on Abigail's face the woman was trying not to laugh. Was this what they'd been discussing when they walked up on them? Somehow, she knew it was.

Heat blazed across her face. Holden had been seen? Who else saw him? And what would happen if they had? Laurel glanced away before saying, "I met him in Missoula before I came here to Willow Creek."

The mirth in Abigail's eyes dimmed. "What? Met who? Holden?

It was Laurel's turn to laugh. "Yes. In a saloon, of all places."

Abigail's eyes widened. "Oh, do tell."

So she did. Laurel laid everything out, every detail she felt comfortable admitting and Abigail was grinning by the time she stopped. "I knew it. I told Morgan something was going on between you two. Holden has never pursued a woman like he has you and I just knew there had to be a reason." She blanched and reached out to grab Laurel's arm. "Not that you aren't beautiful and he wouldn't have eventually tried to win your heart, but Holden is somewhat reserved for the most part. But he wasn't with you."

"You mean he's not always so single-minded and irritating?"

They both shared a laugh before the men approached. Laurel could tell by the look on Morgan's face that he too had been told of their sordid past.

The musicians took a small break, the couples around the clearing gathering in small clusters and whispers grew until it seemed everyone was shouting.

Laurel was half listening to the conversation Holden and Morgan were engaged in when she noticed a man with blond hair walking their way, smiling. A pretty woman clung to his arm, her dark hair pulled up and pinned at the nape of her neck. The man slowed his steps as he drew near and it was Abigail who gasped when she noticed them.

"Emmaline! Tristan! When did you get back?"

The woman smiled prettily and blushed. "We arrived on the stagecoach earlier today."

The men turned and started talking to the man as Abigail embraced the woman in a hug before turning back to face her. "Laurel, this is Emmaline Avery, Tristan's wife." She turned and

LILY GRAISON

nodded to the man with her head. "And that's Tristan, Holden and Morgan's baby brother."

Tristan looked nothing like his brothers. Well, except for his eyes. The same intense Avery blue shined from eyes that made Tristan seem just a little bit more intelligent than the average person. A dimple in his cheek made him appear boyish but Laurel could tell he was closer to her own age. She wasn't sure how old Holden was but she assumed older than her. Looking his way, she thought maybe she should ask. Not that it mattered but she knew so little about the man as it was.

They talked for nearly half an hour, the musicians once again taking up their instruments and when Holden motioned to the dance floor again, Laurel was happy to oblige. Morgan and Tristan escorted their wives to the dance floor as well and Laurel noticed immediately that the musicians had slowed down the pace of the music, a soft melody floating over the area. Laurel sighed as Holden held her close. "I've had fun tonight. Thank you."

"Not as much fun as you'll be having once we can sneak away from here."

Laurel grinned. "You're very sure of yourself, Mr. Avery. I may be too tired by the end of the evening to offer you more than a few goodnight kisses."

In a move so bold Laurel thought for sure her heart would explode right there in front of the whole town, Holden leaned down and kissed her. It was brief but a startled gasp from some-where to Laurel's left let her know someone had seen. She blushed and didn't dare turn her head to see who it was.

"Marry me, Laurel."

Shaking her head while grinning, Laurel stared up at him. "No."

"Why?"

Someone cleared their throat and said, "Because she's already married." The unknown person moved into their line of sight and grabbed Laurel's arm, trying to pull her from Holden's grasp. "Now unhand my wife."

HOLDEN GAPED at the man tugging on Laurel's arm. He wasn't overly tall but the bowler hat on his head made him appear to be. He was dressed in an expensive suit of light brown. He was clean shaven and appeared to be around Holden's own age of thirty.

Reaching out to grasp the man's hand, he pulled it away from Laurel and draped his own arm over her shoulder, tucking her into his body. "I'll advise you not to try that again, mister. Touch my woman and I'll break your arm."

The man glanced from Laurel, then back to him, before he smiled, but there was nothing amusing in the look that settled in his eyes. He straightened his spine, smoothed out the front of his suit jacket and his cheeks turned a slight shade of red before he met his gaze again. "Your woman?"

Holden nodded his head. "Yes."

The man actually laughed while looking between the two of them. He sobered and settled his gaze on Laurel. "Hello, Laurel." He shook his head, the smile on his face as wide as any Holden had ever seen. "I've been searching high and low for you, dove. I was about to give up. Finding you here was just plain dumb luck."

Laurel gaped at the man and Holden's mind was reaching by the time she stuttered out a quiet, "Ethan?"

"Do you know how hard it's been to keep track of you?"

Holden looked down at her, saw her eyes just a bit too wide. Her mouth was opening and closing as if she was trying to speak but nothing was coming out. Turning his attention back to the man, Holden said, "Who are you?"

The man ignored his question, his gaze locked on Laurel. "I've spent the last two months tracking your movements, Laurel. Imagine my surprise in finding you in such a primitive place." He turned his head, gazing around the clearing. "It's quaint but nowhere near your standard of living. I can have us out of here in two days' time. The stagecoach will be back on Tuesday. That will give you ample time to settle any affairs you may have." He eyed Holden again, sneering at him. "Including this one. Now I don't wish for a scene, so say goodnight to your companion and let's go. I'm tired and we've a long journey ahead of us." He held out his hand to her and the silence surrounding them was deafening.

Holden didn't have to look to know everyone in attendance was watching them. The music had stopped and not a voice could be heard, not even the slightest whisper.

Glancing down at Laurel, her complexion looked wane, her eyes seemed much too large for her face and he knew his hold on her was the only thing keeping her upright. "Laurel? Do you know this man?"

She blinked, a soft sigh escaping her throat before she nodded her head, her gaze still locked on the man in front of them.

Holden stared at her while the man's words whispered through his head again. *She's already married. Unhand my wife.*

When the implication of his words hit him, the urge to let go of her was great. He wanted to see her face to gauge her reaction more clearly. He tightened his arm around her instead and lifted his head, looking back at the man. "I don't recall catching your name."

He'd seen many arrogant men in his life but something about this one unsettled him. The man lifted his nose a few inches before saying, "Ethan Dearborn, IV." He glanced at Laurel again. "And Laurel is my wife. May I ask who you are?"

Holden ignored the man's question when Laurel moved away from them both, shaking her head so violently, her carefully upswept hair started falling down in places. "I'm not your wife."

Ethan sighed. "A mere technicality. In the eyes of your father, we are indeed married. Now come along. I'm exhausted, and I wish to rest before venturing on."

She turned those large, luminous eyes to him and Holden saw regret shining in them. Up until that very moment, he thought the man was delusional. Now, he wasn't so sure.

He leaned his head to one side, assessing her thoroughly. "Laurel...?"

She blinked, stared at him with such remorse, his heart clenched in his chest. Every conversation he'd ever had with her assaulted him in rapid succession. Their first meeting in the saloon when she claimed all men were untrustworthy to her refusal to let him court her for reasons she still hadn't explained.

But she did finally accept, he thought. The week before he'd made love to her through the night and not once had she offered any resistance. Her reasons for pushing him away had been gone but the look on her face now told him they were back. Whatever made her change her mind was once again an ugly secret between them. A glance to his left and Holden knew the man causing this ruckus was the reason.

"I'm sorry, Holden."

Her softly spoken words were like a knife to the gut. He stared at her, watching as tears filled her eyes and knew, whatever future they may have had together was over now. Someone touched his arm and he turned to see Morgan by his side, Tristan only a step away.

He laughed suddenly as thoughts ran through his head in fast succession. After all the time it took for Alex to accept Laurel and to get her to stop fighting him... now this? He truly did have the worst luck where women were concerned. Maybe he was just doomed to be alone forever. Looking at Laurel's haunted face, he knew he was.

Turning, he walked away. He wasn't sure what was going on but having it displayed in front of the whole town wasn't something anyone wanted, especially him. He made it to the street and waited to see if Laurel and Ethan would follow him but after several long minutes, neither appeared.

Refusing to look over his shoulder for them, he turned toward the livery stable, collected his horse and was mounted, riding away from the stable when he saw them emerge from between the buildings. Ethan had hold of Laurel's arm and the look on her face would haunt him for a lifetime.

LAUREL WAS SO STUNNED she could do nothing but stand on the sidewalk and watch Holden ride away. Her heart was pounding so fast, the rush of blood past her ears was deafening.

Holden's dark, angry gaze was painful to see. He looked betrayed and she knew she should have told him everything. The moment she decided to let her past go and just live her life, she should have told him about Ethan. Now she may not get the chance.

He turned the horse and sent the stallion into a full run. She watched him until the darkness swallowed both horse and man and nothing but dust remained.

Ethan still had hold of her arm and tugging free from him she turned, and sent him a resentful scowl. "How dare you."

His eyes widened. "How dare I?" He looked shocked. "What have I done?" His shoulders sagged as he looked at her, his features crestfallen. "I've been worried sick about you. Tormented by notions that harm may have befallen you."

He rambled for long minutes, every word a lie. Laurel wasn't as naive as the men in her life liked to believe. Her past was lesson enough for her to see through false intentions and as sincere as Ethan seemed to be, his words were false. He cared for nothing but the money in her father's bank account. Money that would be his once he married her. "How did you find me?" she said, interrupting him.

His smile looked sincere and it was hard to tell if it was. She never knew with Ethan. "Someone was snooping into your past. You father got wind of it and sent me everything he'd learned. I've been tracking your movements for the last several months."

That someone he mentioned had to have been Morgan Avery, or at least someone Morgan had check up on her. She should have left the moment Holden told her his brother found information on her.

Raising her gaze to meet his, she exhaled a long breath. "Why are you here? I made myself perfectly clear last time we spoke. I no longer wish to marry you."

His mouth opened and closed a few times before he sighed. "You no longer love me, you mean?" The look that crossed his face made her heart clench. Remorse filled his face and for a split second, she believed him.

"It's all right, Laurel. Love isn't instantaneous. It's built over time and eventually, you'll love me again."

Laurel knew he was wrong about that. Love could happen quickly. It took nothing more than a single glance. A warm smile or a quick laugh. She'd known that night in the saloon back in Missoula that love could happen in an instant but wouldn't admit it. Doing so now left her heart vulnerable but denying it hurt worse than knowing she'd lost Holden because she didn't trust him enough to be truthful with him.

"You made a fool out of me, Laurel."

She focused her attention back on Ethan. "I beg your pardon?"

He glanced down the street to the people milling around town and straightened the front of his suit jacket. "My friends, my family... do you know how embarrassing it was for me to have you run away?"

"I'm sorry, Ethan. I never meant to embarrass you but what did you expect me to do? I may have embarrassed you but you made a fool out of me. I'd say we were even."

He shrugged one shoulder. "I did no such thing. It was all a misunderstanding. And we can clear this whole mess up if you'll just hear me out and come back home with me. Besides, your father misses you."

He reached for her arm again and Laurel knew he'd drag her kicking and screaming all the way back to Seattle if he had to and she wouldn't let that happen. Movement between the buildings caught Laurel's attention and she saw Morgan and Tristan emerge from the shadows. As much as she didn't want to explain anything to Holden's brothers, she didn't want Ethan to force his will on her either. She straightened her spine, crossed the distance between them and laid her hand on Morgan's arm. "Marshal, will you escort me home, please?"

Morgan stared at Ethan for long moments before nodding his head. "It would be my pleasure." He turned, motioned for Abigail and Emmaline, who were hiding between the buildings, and the five of them left without another word. When they reached the end of the street, Morgan stopped in front of his house, opened the gate and ushered them all onto the stone sidewalk leading to the house. "I didn't want him to follow us to the school. You're welcome to stay with us as long as you like."

Abigail led her into the kitchen after entering the house and indicated she take one of the chairs at the table. Laurel sat, sighed and felt old beyond her years.

She watched Abigail flit around the kitchen, setting a pot of water on to boil as Emmaline grabbed cups and saucers and Laurel could almost taste the tea she knew her new friend was brewing.

Not a word was spoken until after the tea had been served and it was Morgan, who now stood in the kitchen doorway, who spoke.

"Is he dangerous, Laurel?"

She shook her head. "No. He's pompous at times and arrogant the rest, but he would never hurt me."

He nodded, satisfied with her answer, and left the room.

It wasn't until Abigail refilled their tea cups after they'd all finished the first cup that Laurel looked up at her. She hadn't said a word, neither had Emmaline, and for that, Laurel was grateful. She'd been expecting questions the moment they entered the house and if anyone deserved an explanation, it was Holden. "He'll never speak to me again," she said, more to herself than to Abigail and Emmaline. She looked up and noticed them both watching her. "Holden, I mean."

Abigail shifted in her seat and sat her cup down. "He will. Once he's had time to think things through, he'll be banging on your door demanding answers." She laughed and reached out, taking Laurel's hand. "Trust me. Those Averys don't know when to quit. He'll be back. He loves you."

Laurel let out an unladylike snort and shook her head. "I think you're confusing desire with love, Abigail. Holden's never said anything of the sort."

"Just because he hasn't told you means nothing. Do you honestly think he would have tried so hard to win you over just for desire? He could bed any number of women." She grinned and took another sip of her tea. "It's not desire that drives him, Laurel, it's you. He loves you. Just wait and see. He'll say it before the week is out."

Laurel wasn't so sure about that. The night she met Holden, he hadn't appeared to be a man looking for love. He was alone in a saloon notorious for their clean girls. If she had to guess, she'd say he was there for one reason and one reason only. To find a bedmate. And she'd supplied that for him without much hesitation.

She'd felt so miserable that night and hoped to drown all her sorrows in a bottle of whiskey. She'd never been much of a drinker and had stood staring into her glass when it was set before her. Then he spoke, the timbre of his voice rattling her clean to the toes. One glance up at his face and it was as if the earth had shifted. The smile on his face said no matter what the problem was, it wasn't the end of the world and he'd been right.

She'd laughed for the first time in months while standing at the bar talking to a man she knew nothing about. A nameless man with a gentle smile and dazzling blue eyes. A man she'd wanted enough to invite into her room and silently longed for him when he left.

Abigail gave her a reassuring smile and shifted her focus on to Emmaline, asking her questions about the trip she and Tristan had taken. Laurel was barely listening but at the mention of gold, she looked up. Emmaline was looking at her, a look in her eye she'd seen before. The girl had gold fever. She'd seen it before in a dozen other towns.

Without excusing herself, she stood, walked through the house and found Morgan and Tristan in the parlor. They stopped talking the moment they saw her. "I'm sorry to interrupt," she said.

"You didn't. We were just talking about Tristan's trip to Idaho."

Laurel smiled. "There's gold in the hills, I hear." At Tristan's amused look, she shrugged one shoulder. "Emmaline and Abigail were talking about it."

Tristan nodded, throwing her a smile.

Inhaling a deep breath, Laurel turned to Morgan. "I appreciate your offer, Morgan, but I think I'd like to go back to the school."

"Are you sure?"

She nodded her head. "Yes. It's been an eventful night and I'm exhausted. I just want to go home, crawl into my own bed and sleep for a week."

She'd been expecting an argument and when Abigail and Emmaline got involved, it grew heated. Questions about Ethan rose and as much as Laurel wanted to answer them all, she couldn't. Holden was the one who needed to hear it. He was the only one who really mattered.

No one was happy about her leaving but Morgan walked her

back to the school anyway, Tristan following behind at a distance to keep a watch and make sure no one was following them. They didn't trust Ethan and she was slightly amused at how cautious they were.

Morgan entered the room in the back of the school first, made sure no one was inside and waited until she'd bolted the door behind her before leaving. She'd seen him linger by the side of the building for a few minutes when she peeked out the window and she knew he'd be close by regardless of what she told him.

She didn't have a doubt in her mind about Ethan. He wouldn't hurt her. Not physically, anyway. He may say things that hurt her feelings but it was nothing she hadn't heard before from her father. The memories of his hurtful words would remain with her always.

Pushing away the depressing thoughts, she removed her dress, got ready for bed and sat down at the table to try and think. She wasn't sure what to do. Her heart told her to dig in her heels and refuse to budge but that scared little girl in her wanted to flee again. To protect her heart at all costs and run.

She stood, fetched water for tea and had drunk two cups before someone beat on the door so loudly, the wood quaked against the frame. Her heart leaped into her throat and she wondered who was on the other side of the door, Holden or Ethan. Not that it mattered. She didn't want to talk to either of them.

Another furious bang and Holden's voice drifted through the wood, her name yelled angrily.

"Laurel! Open the door. I know you're in there."

CHAPTER 9

SWALLOWING to dislodge the lump in her throat, or was it really her heart, she stood, crossed the room and unbolted the door. Holden barged in, slammed the door back shut with one foot and sent her a look that chilled her to the bone.

"You're married?" He shook his head, laughed and jerked his hat off his head, tossing it across the room. "All this time I've been making a fool of myself asking you to marry me and you already have a husband?"

She tried to speak but he shoved away from the wall, paced the length of her small room and glared at her on every pass, grumbling and voicing his displeasure. "Why, Laurel? Was all this some game to you? Did you enjoy seeing me grovel like an idiot, beg you to marry me like some love-sick fool knowing nothing I ever said or did would make you change your mind?"

Ten minutes of listening to him rant and rave and Laurel leaned back against the wall, watching him make laps over her rug and even managed to hide a yawn when his back was turned. She wasn't about to complain because of his behavior. Truth be known, she was happy he even bothered to come back. She didn't think he would. Once Ethan started spouting his lies, Laurel thought for sure Holden would have gone back to the ranch and never thought of her again.

She was contemplating the split-ends of her hair when she noticed Holden had stopped yelling. She looked up, saw him on the other side of the room staring at her. "What?"

"Have you heard anything I've said?"

"Umm...most of it." She bit her lip to keep from smiling.

Holden narrowed his eyes, leaning his head to one side. "Which parts?"

Laurel straightened and dropped her braid. "I heard the part where you think I've been lying to you. Which I haven't done. I also heard something about Maggie and how she'd never deceived you and the fact that I did was unforgivable." She met his gaze and let him see how much that statement hurt. "I've never lied to you, Holden. I've been honest with you from the beginning. I told you the day I brought Alexandra home, and I found out you lived here, that nothing would ever become of this. You were the one who insisted. You were the one who wouldn't give up. And this is the reason I've told you no so adamantly."

"Because you were already married?"

"No!" She took a deep breath, regretting she'd yelled. "We're not married." Her cheeks heated and without being told, she knew her face was red. "I left him at the altar."

Holden raised one eyebrow. "So you agreed to marry him, then left?" At her nod, he said, "Why?"

She hated retelling the story. It was humiliating to rehash it all, to even remember how she'd been used. Holden crossed the room, stopped in front of her and hooked a finger under her chin, lifting her head so she'd look at him. "You know what? I don't want to know. It doesn't matter." He stared down at her, the truth of his words shining in his eyes. "I love you, Laurel. I've loved you from the moment you smiled at me in that noisy saloon in Missoula. I wanted you forever the first time I kissed you. I still want you, regardless if you have a husband or a fiancé you left at the altar or whoever the hell he is. I want you for my wife and I'll not take no for an answer."

Abigail's words filled her head again and it was all Laurel could do to keep from crying. She stared up at Holden, the admission of her own feelings on the tip of her tongue but fear kept her silent. Ethan claimed to love her too and he'd ripped her heart into shreds. Could she take that chance again? Did she want to?

She blinked away the stinging in her eyes. "How do I know you won't hurt me a year from now? Or five years from now?"

He narrowed his eyes at her and leaned his head to one side. "Define hurt?"

She started to answer but he cut her off before she had a chance.

"Will I get on your nerves and make you mad? Probably. Will I irritate you to the point you'll make me sleep outside with the horses? More than likely. Will I beat you, betray you, take you for granted or toss you aside? Never. I love you, Laurel. I'd never do anything to purposely hurt you. That's a promise."

Lord she wanted to believe him. Wanted with all her heart to let her guard down and just let what happens, happen. "Will you take other women to your bed?"

He looked shocked by the question but shook his head and said, "No. I don't want other women. I want you."

"But what about later? Say, years from now when I'm old and fat. Will you want someone else then?"

Staring down at her, something in his eyes told her he knew why she was so fearful of commitment. He smiled, lowered his head until his lips lingered just above her own. "I'll never be unfaithful to you, Laurel. You have my word."

She sighed, the tension in her body draining as he closed the distance and kissed her. "No more secrets, Laurel. No more hiding from me." Wrapping his arms around her, he smiled and hugged her to him. "I've been nothing but honest with you from the beginning. I want you. Always have."

She nodded, relief filling her to the point of exhaustion. "What about Ethan?"

"What about him?" he asked. "Do you want to marry him?"

"No. I would have never left home if I had."

"Then there's nothing to worry about where he is concerned."

"He's not going to leave, Holden."

"Well, that depends on what you do between now and the next time you see him."

"Meaning?"

He grinned and hooked a finger under her chin so she couldn't look away. "Will you marry me?"

She shouldn't have been shocked by the question, he'd only asked her the same thing a dozen times before but for the first time, she wanted to say yes without hesitation. Looking up at him, she smiled and said, "No."

His grin widened, the hand under her chin lowering to the top of her nightgown, tugging on the ribbon holding it closed. "So you do want to marry Ethan."

"No."

His deft fingers freed her breasts before sliding into the front of her gown. "You don't want Ethan. You don't want me. What is it you want, Miss Montgomery?" He tweaked one nipple, causing a moan to spill from her lips. Her eyes closed, her bottom lip tucked between her teeth. "Marry me, Laurel, and the problem with Ethan will go away."

She opened her eyes and looked up at him when he tugged her gown down over her shoulders, the material pooling at her feet. A bit of mischief lurked behind his eyes but she saw his desire for her there, too.

Holden Avery wasn't like any other man she'd ever known. He

was a breed of man truly unique. He trusted and forgave with a blink of the eye and she'd be a fool to let him go. So why couldn't she say yes?

He gave her little time to contemplate an answer. He lowered his head, his lips tickling a path across her breasts before sucking one taunt nipple into his mouth. Laurel closed her eyes, let her head fall back against the wall and just enjoyed the sensations he elicited.

His lips burned a trail between her breast and her pulse leaped when he knelt before her, untying her bloomers, before kissing the soft skin of her belly. He pulled her bloomers down to join her gown near her ankles, his mouth venturing lower, his tongue hot and wet on her hip. When he reached the juncture between her legs, her knees went weak.

Parting her folds, he kissed and suckled her, his tongue burrowing into her and greedily taking what he wanted. He lifted her left leg, placed it over his shoulder and didn't stop licking her until tremors caused her limbs to shake, small anguished sounds tore from her throat and she'd grabbed his head with both hands, to push him away or pull him closer, she didn't know. She shifted her hips, brought him closer to where she needed him and cried out as she climaxed, her body convulsing so hard she was bucking against the wall.

When she was spent, sucking in lungs full of air, he lowered her leg. His hands slid up her body, his lips following the trail he left before he let go of her. Hearing a rustle of fabric, she opened her eyes, and watched him remove his clothes as his gaze bore into her own. When they both stood naked, he smiled, ran the back of one finger down her cheek and wrapped his other arm around her. "I'm not leaving until you say yes."

Picking her up, he carried her to the bed, positioned himself between her thighs and slid into her body with such aching slowness, she thought she'd die from the waiting. The pace he set was meant to torture, she was sure, and he never let his gaze leave her own.

It took only minutes for her body to heat again, for small tingles to course through her limbs and she clung to him, her nails biting into his shoulders. When he said, "Marry me," Laurel's heart felt so light, she thought it would burst. Tears burned her eyes, her arms around his shoulders tightening and the word yes was on the tip of her tongue. She climaxed moments later, her tears spilling forth to mingle with her cries of ecstasy, Holden's own hoarse cry joining hers.

When he stilled and collapsed beside her on the bed, Laurel could do nothing but stare up at the ceiling and try to remember how to breathe. Small shocks of pleasure rode her limbs, an incessant throb pulsing through her body letting her know she was alive and Holden's arm, so strong and steady, holding her close to his side.

She sighed, and then turned her head to where he lay. He was watching her, love shining in his eyes. "I'm scared."

"Of what?"

"Of getting hurt again."

Holden shifted, pulling her closer to his side and rested his chin on the top of her head. "Tell me about Ethan."

Laurel toyed with the hair on his chest while thinking. "Our marriage was arranged by my father before I left for college. Ethan saw no need for me to continue my studies because he saw me as doing nothing after marriage but taking care of him, our home and any children we would have and he told me repeatedly I couldn't go away to school. I refused to be stopped. I wanted more. I wanted to teach and I wasn't going to let him stop me. With my father's persuasion, Ethan relented and I left for Boston and got my degree."

She wrapped her arm around Holden, burying her face into his neck and let memories that still caused pain to engulf her. "He was such a gentleman. So dashing. He courted me with a flourish no one in Seattle had seen in years. During my time in Boston, gifts and letters would show up weekly. When I returned home, he produced lavish gifts, took me on picnics and even hired a circus to set up their tents on the outskirts of town to celebrate my birthday." She exhaled a breath and smiled when Holden's arms wrapped around her tighter. "He told me he loved me, that he'd do anything in his power to make me happy and when he wasn't courting me, he was doing all he could to help my father. Ethan is quite adapt at turning nothing into something extraordinary and with his help, my father's business grew in a matter of months. Profits were up and everyone was happy. Most of all, me.

My mother died when I was thirteen so it was just my father and me living in a monstrosity of a house. I was lonely for the most part because father didn't approve of most of the girls I knew. When Ethan came along, he swept me off my feet, I guess you could say. When I returned from college, we set a wedding date. I gave myself to him that very night as if we were already married."

Leaning back, Laurel looked up, wanting to see Holden's face. "Two weeks before our wedding, I stopped by Ethan's office in town to invite him to lunch. No one was in the outer offices so I let myself in to his personal space and I saw him with his receptionist. They didn't see me and they were talking so I didn't want to interrupt. When Ethan kissed her, I was so shocked, I couldn't move."

Holden kissed her forehead, his hand moving to caress her cheek. "What happened after that?"

"I only caught snatches of the conversation. My ears were ringing by that point. It felt as if I was standing outside my body watching everything unfold and I was just a bystander. Ethan and his receptionist were laughing and kissing, they looked more intimate than he and I ever did, and I felt like such a fool. After giving myself to him, ruining myself for him... I knew Ethan didn't love me as I watched them together. He loved my father's bank account and I was the easiest way to get to it."

Rolling onto her back, Laurel sighed again. "I left and went straight home, told my father what I'd seen and he looked me in the face and told me to never repeat what I'd told him. That it was a man's right to do as he pleased. That if Ethan wanted a mistress, or a whole host of them, it was his privilege to have one. I thought of my mother then, of how unhappy she looked when I saw her sitting alone in the garden before she died and knew then that my father had his own indiscretions. My father had a mistress and my mother died feeling as betrayed as I did. I refused to live the rest of my life in such a manner."

Holden shifted and leaned up on one elbow, looking down at her. "Did you not call off the wedding?"

"I tried. My father refused to let me. He said he'd already paid for everything and if I wanted to remain in his will, I'd do exactly as he said." She laughed bitterly and shook her head. "I think there was some sort of business arrangement between the two of them. Something they were both getting out of our marriage and I saw no way out. I discreetly sold everything of value I had and tucked it all away into a purse I kept pinned to the inside of my chemise and waited for the first opportunity I had to leave. As luck would have it, I was never alone until the day of the wedding. I told my attendants I needed to use the privy before dressing and the moment they left the room, I snuck out the window and ran. I've been running for the last twelve months."

"Are you going to run again?"

Looking up at him, Laurel could see he was scared she'd do just that. She also knew she wouldn't make it very far. He'd come after her. She knew he would without being told. The thought thrilled, and terrified, her. "How far would you let me get?"

He grinned, his eyes lighting up. "About as far as the end of town." He leaned down and kissed her, his tongue dipping into her mouth to taste her. "If you never offer me anything but clandestine meetings, then that's all I'll ever take from you, but I want more. I want you to be my wife. To share my life with you and to help me raise Alex. To fill my house with kids and laughter and to grow old with you. If you can't give me either, then just say so and I'll leave you alone. It'll kill me to do it but I will."

He kissed her again, softly, and so slow it was agonizing. Her heart screamed out to say yes. That she'd marry him come morning but that part of her that was still scared of being hurt refused to budge.

"You don't trust me not to hurt you, do you?"

She sighed and met his gaze. "I trust you, Holden. I just don't trust myself not to always wonder when you'll betray me. I can't live like that. It isn't fair to either of us."

"Then how can I convince you?"

"I don't know."

HOLDEN WAS GONE when she woke, regardless of his promise not to leave until she accepted his marriage proposal. Sunlight was streaming in the window through her curtain and Laurel laid there for another half an hour watching shadows dance across the walls.

Her body still tingled in places. Holden had made love to her half the night. He hadn't brought up the subject of marriage again after their talk and she was grateful. As much as it hurt to tell him no, hearing him ask it and not answer, yes, was torture. It would solve most of her problems by saying yes but she couldn't. A small part of her still didn't trust men. Even though she told Holden she trusted him, she knew she didn't. Not truly. She would have said yes if she did. All men had the ability to hurt her and after being treated so badly by Ethan, it would take more than pretty words and stolen kisses in the night to change that.

Climbing from the bed, she washed and dressed, taking stock of her small food pantry. She'd have to go to the mercantile today to replenish her food stuff. She grabbed a small basket from under the bed, grabbed her reticule and ventured across town.

Mrs. Jenkins smiled at her as she entered the store. Two other women were near the back of the store and their hushed whispers died the moment they saw her. They both smiled but Laurel knew they were just being polite. Apparently the scene from last night was today's hottest gossip.

She returned the ladies' smiles and browsed the isles, keeping her eyes downcast. The whispers started again and Laurel ignored them best she could. The bell above the door clinked as someone entered and warm welcomes were issued to the newcomer. Laurel looked up and saw Holden's sister-in-law, Sarah, and his twin brother, Colt, walking her way.

"Good morning," Sarah said, smiling. "I stopped by the school for a visit and was disappointed when you didn't answer your door. I knew there was only a few places you could be and here you are."

Laurel looked up at Colt, amazed to see a man who looked just like Holden standing there with his arm around another woman. Sarah was obviously pleased to have her husband's undivided attention and she smiled at them both before securing her basket at the crook of her arm. "Good morning."

Sarah gave Colt a brief look. "We wanted to invite you to supper. We don't have many guests out at the ranch and we've not had time enough to sit and talk. I was hoping you'd join us so we could get better acquainted."

Laurel wasn't sure why Sarah had a sudden urge to be better acquainted but something in Colt's eyes told her it had everything to do with Holden. Just thinking of him sent her heart fluttering and it must have shown on her face. Sarah's smile widened and with a simple nod of her head, Colt leaned down, kissed Sarah on the cheek, said, "I'll see you soon, Laurel," and left.

When the bell above the door chimed again, Sarah, who was still standing there smiling at her said, "So, is six this evening good for you?"

"Today?" Laurel swallowed the trepidation she felt. "I'm not sure today is such a good time."

"Why not?"

Why? Had Sarah not heard the latest gossip? Did she not know Ethan, her ex-fiancé, was in town and trying to get her to go home with him?

Sarah took a step closer and leaned down so no one else would hear her. "Don't worry about the gossips. They'd all shrivel up and die if they didn't have anything to talk about but don't let that keep you from enjoying your life. It's much too short to just let it pass you by." She straightened, smiled again and laid one hand on her rounded belly. "I must go. If I don't get food into me every two hours, I end up so sick I can barely stand but please say you'll come tonight."

Laurel wanted to refuse but Sarah looked genuinely happy to extend the invitation, she hated to refuse. "Where do you live?"

The smile Sarah graced her with would have lit a starless night. "I've already made arrangements for you to be brought to the house. Just be ready to leave by five this evening. It'll take a while to reach the ranch."

Sarah said her goodbyes and as Laurel watched her leave, wondered who would be taking her out to Sarah and Colt's home. One person came to mind and as much as she wanted to see Holden again, she dreaded it just the same. He'd ask her to marry him again and telling him no was getting hard to do. She hoped he'd tire of asking her soon because her heart broke just a little bit more every time she told him no.

She made quick work of her shopping, the things that wouldn't fit into her basket were to be delivered around noon and she was on her way back to the school when she heard her name being called. The voice shouting it sent a tremor up her spine.

Stopping, and turning to look behind her, Laurel saw Ethan running up the sidewalk toward her, a bouquet of flowers clasped in one hand. As much as she didn't want to talk to him, she was through running.

When he reached her, he smiled, wiped sweat from his brow and looked up into the early morning sunlight. "Pretty day we're having." His smile widened. "Not nearly as fetching as you are, though. You look like a ray of sunshine."

"Stop trying to flatter me. It no longer works."

He looked taken aback. "I wasn't trying to flatter you. I was just stating the obvious. You look beautiful. You always do."

Laurel exhaled a deep breath. "What do you want?"

"A chance to talk to you about what you think you saw back in Seattle."

"There's nothing to talk about," Laurel said. "I know what I saw. I know what I heard. I know how I feel. I'll not be used and betrayed by anyone, Ethan, least of all you, so if you'll excuse me, I have things to do today." She turned and left him standing there gaping at her. She'd only taken half a dozen steps when he said, "Holden Avery. That's the man you were with last night."

Laurel stopped and turned back to face him. He was smiling.

"I hear he's been chasing after you since the moment you got into town." Ethan laughed and shook his head. "Heard he's been seen sneaking away from the school, where you live, in the predawn hours as well." Leaning his head to one side, he narrowed his eyes. "It's a bit silly to accuse me of sleeping around when you're sneaking around yourself. Funny, I thought for sure I was the only man you'd ever been with but seeing how you've taken up with this Avery character, I have to wonder just what kind of woman you are."

Laurel's temper flared so hot, she thought for sure she'd catch fire. She closed the distance between them, stood nose to nose with him and stared him in the eye. "What I do is my own business and I'll invite anyone I feel like to my bed. You lost that privilege when you slept with half the town behind my back. Do you honestly think I was stupid enough to think your receptionist was the only one? My father isn't the only person who has resources. I know of your indiscretions, Ethan, all of them, and believe me, I look like a saint compared to you."

He said nothing but the smile that curved his mouth said enough. He wasn't even going to deny it. Laurel took three steps back, gaining some distance between them and narrowed her eyes at him. "I want you to leave, Ethan. I'll not be returning to Seattle. This is my home now and I'll not be leaving. Now, if you'll excuse me, I have things to do."

She left without another word and thankfully he didn't try to stop her. His laughter followed her down the street and when he yelled, "This isn't over, Laurel," she quickened her steps. She made it all the way back to the school before tears of frustration burnt her eyes and spilled over her lashes. She bolted the door to her room, dropped her basket to the floor and cried until she thought she'd be sick.

All she'd ever wanted was someone to love her. To adore her like she thought her father adored her mother but even that had been a lie. She wasn't even sure true love was possible anymore. Not the kind she'd read about in books. The kind that lasted forever and was soul-deep. Maybe her expectations were just too high. That she should be happy with what life offered her and be satisfied with it.

Her thoughts went to Holden then. Fate had presented him to her on a warm fall evening in Missoula and then again when she reached Willow Creek. Maybe what she'd been looking for was right in front of her and all she had to do was reach out and take it. The fear in her heart was still there but closing her eyes and seeing Holden's face in her mind's eye, she smiled. He wouldn't hurt her, just as he'd said, so what was holding her back?

Wiping her face with the back of her hand, she sniffled, picked her basket up and blew out an exhausted breath. She had a lot to think about and the next time she saw Holden, she'd give him an answer, one way or the other.

CHAPTER 10

HOLDEN HEARD the wagon before he saw it and his pulse leaped the moment he looked out toward the road leading to Colt and Sarah's place. Morgan and Abigail, along with their daughter Elizabeth, were heading toward his brother's and even though the distance was too great to make her out clearly, he could see Laurel on the seat beside Abigail.

He watched them pass the house. Colt had invited them to supper as well and Alex had run to their house hours ago to help watch Emma so Sarah could prepare things. He still hadn't made the slightest attempt to wash and change his clothes. Watching that wagon pass the house, he wasn't sure he should.

After weeks of trying to get through to Laurel, he now knew what was holding her back. Why she wouldn't commit to any sort of relationship and as much as he wanted her for his wife, he wasn't sure she'd ever accept his proposal. Now with Ethan in town, he feared she'd leave Willow Creek with her ex-fiancé. He wasn't sure what he'd do if she did.

The idea of losing her had invaded his thoughts since the night before. Ever since Ethan showed up at the dance and said Laurel was his wife. He could still hear the smug tone in the man's voice and thoughts of violence caused his fists to clench. He'd waited too long to find Laurel to let her go but if she didn't want him...

He sighed. They were good together. The sex alone was enough to leave him feeling dazed but it wasn't even the prospect of having a willing woman in his bed night after night that made him crave her. It was her. The way her face turned pink when she was embarrassed. The smiles he knew she only offered him. That soft, tinkling laughter that worked its way into his soul and made him feel ten years younger. The way she looked at him, her whiskey colored eyes drinking him in and making him feel like there wasn't another man around for miles.

He'd been imagining a life with her since leaving Missoula, even more so when she turned up in Willow Creek and he knew if she refused to marry him, he'd spend the rest of his life wanting her. He may marry someone else someday in the future but it would only be to give Alex a mother.

Pete, one of the ranch hands, called his name and he turned back to the barn. He still had work to do, regardless of his supper plans. Walking back toward the barn, something out of the corner of his eye caught his attention. He stopped, looked toward the tree line to the left of the barn and squinted into the dying sun. Nothing but the tree branches moved and he shrugged off the feeling of being watched before walking into the barn. He nodded to the men already there and grabbed the bail of hay he'd dropped when he saw the wagon.

Tossing it to Pete, he turned to grab another and tried to put Laurel out of his mind. Maybe if he just gave her some space, stopped badgering her about marrying him, she'd come to a decision about them.

⚜

THE AVERY CLAN had been pleasant supper companions, even

Alexandra, but Holden's absence had been felt to degrees Laurel wasn't sure how to process. She missed him and knowing she was probably the reason he hadn't shown up left her feeling dejected.

The ladies had moved to the parlor, a spacious room with a warm fire burning, lace curtains at the windows and rich fabrics covering the furniture.

Alexandra was in the play room with Abigail and Sarah's daughters and the men were on the porch discussing things no woman cared to hear about, she was sure.

The chatter was lighthearted and Laurel listened as she sipped her tea. Emmaline seemed to open up and talk more since the topic of conversation was the new house being built at the edge of the property. Laurel had seen it when they rode under the arched entryway leading to the Avery Ranch. Colt and Sarah's house, a two-story structure almost the size of the main house, was nestled behind the creek in a thicket of trees that was sure to be protected from the summer sun by acres of shade.

The conversation had stopped and Laurel glanced up, startling a little when she noticed everyone was staring at her. "I'm sorry. Did you say something?"

Sarah smiled. "I said Holden will be here soon."

Abigail nodded, confirming Sarah's statement. "He's probably just tied up with work. He doesn't make the ranch hands do anything he isn't willing to help with himself. They're probably knee deep mucking out stalls or storing hay."

Laurel didn't reply but her conscious was eased a bit. Thinking Holden was working was better than thinking he was avoiding her. The silence was deafening and again, everyone was still looking at her. Laurel knew they wanted something, she just wasn't sure what that was. Setting her cup down, she folded her hands in her lap and smiled. "What is it you want to know, ladies?

They actually blushed, threw covert glances to each other and it was Abigail who spoke. "We were just wondering about the man from the dance last night."

She should have seen it coming and was surprised they hadn't asked before now. Telling them nothing would be easier than rehashing it all but out of everyone in Willow Creek, this set of ladies were the only ones she felt she could call friends, as tenuous as their relationship was.

She didn't go into as much detail as she had with Holden, but she gave them the gist of it and it satisfied their curiosity. They asked a few questions, which she answered, and when Sarah asked what she planned to do now, Laurel was at a loss for words.

"I really don't know," she said. "I'll not be leaving with him, if that's what you mean."

Abigail leaned forward in her seat. "Accepting Holden's marriage proposal would settle it once and for all."

The others agreed, and so did Laurel to a certain extent. Marrying Holden would solve a lot of her problems but it brought others to mind as well. The main one being, would he betray her like Ethan did?

The answer to that whispered in her mind the moment she thought it. He wouldn't. For all his irritating, stubborn ways, he was an honest man. He loved with his whole heart and she knew he'd love her until his dying breath. So why was she still refusing to marry him?

The men were returning, their voices carrying through the house as they entered through the front door. A gust of chill wind followed in their wake and when Laurel turned to look at them, her heart stuttered to a stop before pounding against her ribcage. Holden was standing in the foyer smiling at her. He removed his hat, ran splayed fingers through his hair and said hello to the other ladies in the room before turning to face her.

"Would you like to take a ride with me?"

"A ride?" Laurel asked. "Where to?"

He shrugged. "No place in particular." He glanced to the others and Laurel noticed his cheeks were red. She'd never seen the man blush but there was a first time for everything.

His gaze held hers to the point her pulse was leaping and she found it hard to breathe. She smiled at him, watching his eyes sparkle from nothing more than that one small gesture on her part and the answer to the question she'd been asking herself all night became clear. She loved this man, had since meeting him and, just as he'd told her so many times, she wanted him. For no other reason than just being near him made her day brighter, made life worth living.

She excused herself and crossed the room to where he stood. "Lead the way, Mr. Avery."

He smiled at her and reached for her coat after she pulled it from a peg on the wall near the door and helped her slip it on. After she'd buttoned it, he escorted her outside and Laurel stopped at the top of the steps.

When he'd asked her to take a ride with him, she'd assumed he meant in a wagon or a buggy of some sort but there was nothing out front but his black stallion, the creature looking up at them both, as if impatient to get moving again.

Holden took her hand, led her down the steps and before she could ask him about their mode of transportation, he grabbed her around the waist and lifted her onto the horse and climbing on behind her.

He'd sat her sidesaddle and she turned her head to look at him once he grabbed the reins and guided the horse toward the creek. "I missed you at supper."

He looked surprised, and pleased, by the admission. "I tried like hell to get finished in time but with winter coming on, there's more work than there is daylight to get it all done." He closed his arms around her tighter, pulling her closer into his body. "Figured a sunset stroll through the valley would be more pleasant than supper anyway. I don't have to share you out here."

Laurel leaned into him and smiled. "I prefer this myself," she said, craning her neck and giving him a soft kiss. When she pulled back enough to see his face, she knew she'd made the right decision. The only thing she had to do now was tell him she'd marry him.

They crossed the creek in front of Colt and Sarah's house and meandered along the shallow creek bed for long minutes, the dying sun sending splashes of red and purples chasing each other across the sky. The mountains in the distance were awash with color, the trees climbing their peeks painted in orange, yellow and crimson.

Neither spoke until Holden halted the horse, pulling him to a stop at the far end of the ranch. Laurel didn't know how much of the valley was Avery land but from where they were, she could see the main two-story ranch house, Colt and Sarah's place off in the distance, and the construction of Tristan and Emmaline's future home.

The fencing that surrounded the area looked to run for miles in either direction. She imagined what it would look like come spring, the land dotted with horses and ponies, the grass vibrant green with wildflowers covering the valley in a rainbow of color. It was stunning, this isolated stretch of land in Montana.

"What are you thinking?"

Laurel smiled and continued to look out across the valley. "I was thinking how beautiful this would be come spring."

He shifted on the horse, wrapping her more securely in his arms. "It is." He settled his chin on her head, sighed contently, and didn't speak for long moments.

When he said, "It means nothing, though, if there's no one here to share it with," Laurel's heart skipped a beat and she smiled, silently encouraging him to ask her to marry him again, just one more time. She turned her head, gazed up at him and lifted her hand, caressing his cheek. "Life is nothing with no one to share it with."

The look he gave her heated her skin, chased away the chill mountain air and warmed her clear to her toes. He smiled, his eyes lighting up for an instant before he leaned down to kiss her, his mouth hard and firm against her own. Raising her arms, Laurel hugged him to her, forced her tongue into his mouth and kissed him with all the love she felt for him while the horse danced under them. They were both panting for breath when they reluctantly pulled away from each other. His smile was still in place and the happiness shining in his eyes let her know she'd made the right decision.

A flicker of light out of the corner of her eye caught her attention and she looked over his shoulder, squinting. The main ranch house was to their back now and it took her a moment to realize what she was seeing. She gasped, pulled away from him and shouted, "Fire!"

CHAPTER 11

THEY RACED into the yard and the horse had barely come to a stop before Holden jumped to the ground and was running. The barn was ablaze, the ranch hands running with buckets of water and Laurel slid from the horse's back, grabbed the reins and pulled him away, toward the house. She was tying the reins to a post in front of the house when Holden ran into the barn, mindless of the flames licking at the sides of the structure.

Holden's father, James, walked out onto the porch and his eyes were wide, a frightened look covering his face. Laurel had never spoken to the man, and had barely made his acquaintance at the picnic Holden invited her to, but she hurried up the steps and grabbed hold of his arm just as he was about to venture down into the yard. "We best stay here, Mr. Avery. Let the ranch hands handle this one."

He looked over at her as if he'd just then noticed she was standing there. He held her gaze for long moments and Laurel couldn't be sure, but she thought he was taking her measure. Whatever he saw must have pleased him because he gave her a curt nod and eased away from the steps.

They stood by the front door of the house, watching as man

after man raced into the burning barn. With every passing second, Laurel's pulse beat faster. The acrid scent of smoke filled the air and when the last of the sun dipped down behind the mountain, the red haze from the flames lit up the night sky.

Colt, Morgan and Tristan raced into the yard, all three of them jumping from their horses much in the same manner as Holden had, their horses left unattended. Laurel told James to stay where he was before rushing down the stairs to collect the animals' reins and tying them where she'd left Holden's horse. The women were following close behind the men in the wagon, and soon the entire Avery clan was there, the men rushing to save the animals trapped in the barn, the women carrying their babies up onto the porch, their fretful cries unheard against the roar of the fire.

Alexandra was still in the yard, staring off toward the barn and it wasn't until she turned her head to look back at the house that Laurel started down the stairs.

"Where's my pa?"

"He's saving the horses," Laurel shouted, hoping the girl could hear her over the noise.

Alexandra's eyes widened moments before she turned back to the barn. When Laurel reached the last step, the girl ran, screaming for her father.

Laurel hadn't had the need to run in longer than she could remember but catching Alexandra was harder than it should have been. She reached her at the edge of the barnyard, wrapping her arms around her waist as the frightened horses ran from the barn and past them as if they weren't standing there.

The heat was intense, the smoke breath-stealing and Laurel pulled at Alexandra, tugging her backwards and away from the blaze as the girl screamed and fought her.

They both toppled to the ground and Laurel thought they'd both be trampled by the horses that were trying to escape the blaze. She struggled to stay calm, regained her feet while holding onto Alexandra, and picked the girl up awkwardly, running back toward the house.

"Let me go! My pa's in there!"

"I know, sweetheart. But he can't get the horses if he has to worry about you."

Alexandra Avery was made of sterner stuff than most children Laurel had encountered but seeing her now, crying and trying to get to her father, let her know that deep down, she was just a frightened little girl like other ten year olds were. Laurel struggled to hold her and ended up back on her knees, her arms wrapped around Alexandra in a death grip. "He'll be fine, Alexandra. Please, stop fighting. He'll be all right."

It wasn't until that last, stuttered sentence, that Laurel realized she was crying as hard as Alexandra was. She held the girl to her, stared into the barn and willed Holden to come out.

The fire had leapt to the roof and was working its way to the other side of the building. Laurel could see faint shapes inside, moving, but she couldn't be sure it wasn't just smoke. She'd never been inside the barn but could only imagine the amounts of dry hay stored there. The entire thing was a death trap.

Thoughts of Holden filled her head as she sat there on the ground with Alexandra watching that building burn. Things she wished she'd said, done, when she'd had the chance. As the men inside came rushing out, their voices carrying on the wind, everyone froze, watching in horror as the left side of the building collapsed. Alexandra screamed and Laurel bit her tongue until she tasted blood to keep from doing the same.

Alexandra struggled, flinging her arms, her legs thrashing as she tried to break Laurel's hold, and they were both crying in earnest by the time Holden emerged from the building. Laurel's relief was so profound, she loosened her grip on Alexandra and the girl jumped to her feet and ran.

Holden staggered away from the blaze, collapsing to his hands and knees coughing. His brothers were behind him, all of them

LILY GRAISON

covered in black soot. Laurel struggled to her feet, staring at Holden as he lifted his head in time to catch Alexandra, who flung herself at him. He sat up on his knees, wrapped the girl in his embrace as his gaze sought her out. When she caught his eye, Laurel sucked in a breath and ran to him, a flash of white shining on his face as he smiled.

She fell to her knees in front of him, wrapped her arms around his neck and the three of them sat for long minutes, the barn burning behind them. "Are you hurt?" Laurel asked, her voice scratchy.

Holden shook his head. "No, I'm fine."

He was covered in soot, his clothes singed in places and Laurel pulled back from him enough to see his face. She wiped a hand across his cheeks, smearing sweat and soot, and kissed him without a care for the mess. "I love you," she whispered against his mouth.

He laughed, the sound coming out rough and raw. "I know you do, woman. And it's about damn time you admitted it."

Alexandra's face was buried against Holden's shoulder but she lifted her head then and looked up at her. She didn't say a word, the look on her face solemn.

Everyone moved to the house, Morgan, Colt and Tristan all being coddled by their wives and Laurel helped Holden to his feet. They walked back across the yard, Holden's arms draped around both her and Alexandra's shoulders. She sat him on the steps, watched as Alexandra nestled into his side and left them there, venturing into the house and searching every room until she entered the kitchen.

She found a water bucket, filled it from the pump over the sink and wrapped her fingers around as many handled cups as she could before walking back through the house and outside.

With the help of Abigail and Emmaline, they spent the next hour making sure everyone had water, the small burns they'd suffered cleaned and when the ranch hands made their way slowly back toward the bunk house, Laurel wiped a hand over her brow. The Avery clan was still there on the porch, Sarah sitting in one of the rockers with Emma and Elizabeth perched on her disappearing lap due to her swelling belly. The men lingered around the railing, still coughing occasionally, dirty from head to toe and smelling of smoke. The barn had collapsed, the fire only smoldering but it would take clear to morning before the flames died completely.

Morgan, Colt and Tristan collected their families and after a few quiet words with Holden, they all loaded back into the wagon the women had used to bring them to the main house, the men collecting their horses. Laurel watched them but turned her attention to James when he took her by the elbow. "Take me to my room," he said, his gruff voice startling her. "I'm ready for bed."

Holden turned his head to look at them and raised one eyebrow before smiling. Laurel shrugged one shoulder at him before opening the door and helping James into the house.

"There you go, Mr. Avery," she said, as they reached his bedroom door. "Is there anything I can get you?"

He didn't turn to look at her but said, "No. Go see to my boy, though. He looks like hell."

Laurel grinned when James shut the door in her face, his words still playing in her mind. She turned, walked back out onto the porch and noticed everyone was gone. It was then she realized her ride home was as well and Holden was in no shape to venture into town, regardless of what he'd think about the matter.

His black stallion was still tied to the post by the house, the other horses left to wander in the pasture. She wasn't an exceptional rider but if one of the ranch hands couldn't see her back to town, she was positive she could make it there on that stallion with little problem.

Holden stood with the help of the hand rail on the steps and he waited for Alexandra to stand before he turned to the house. "Let's go wash up," he told her. "And get you ready for bed."

There was a refusal on Alexandra's tongue, her mouth open to voice it but a glance at her father stopped it. She nodded her head and, holding on to his arm—to help him up the stairs or from her own fear of letting him go, Laurel didn't know which—they took the stairs one at a time until they reached the top.

Alexandra reached for the door and it wasn't until she moved away from Holden's side that Laurel noticed his shirt was singed, his skin red and irritated. Her eyes widened but one look from Holden and she bit her tongue. He hadn't said a word when they were cleaning wounds and she figured Alexandra was the reason. She was already scared. If she knew he was hurt, she'd never settle down.

"Alex, go on up and get ready for bed. I'll be up to tuck you in once I've had a chance to clean up."

The girl looked ready to refuse and Laurel smiled, extended her hand and said, "Come on. I'll come with you while your father washes the soot off of himself."

Alexandra looked as if she wanted to decline the offer but didn't. She didn't take Laurel's offered hand, either, but she didn't say anything when Laurel followed her up the stairs.

She entered the first room on the right and Laurel smiled as she took in the space. It was nothing like she imagined it would be. It was decorated in pink, and lace curtains hung at the windows, and Laurel was taken aback by the sight. Alexandra tossed her a look over her shoulder and shrugged, as if to say, she knew the room wasn't her.

Laurel crossed the threshold, pushed the door shut and walked to the bed, folding down the blankets as Alexandra kicked off her boots and started unbuttoning her shirt. She undressed in silence and Laurel kept her back to her until Alexandra said, "Okay. You can look."

Dressed in a long white nightgown, her pigtails trailing over her shoulders, she looked every bit the girl she was. Laurel looked to the dresser, saw her hairbrush and crossed the space toward it. "Let's get your hair brushed out and rebraided, then you can climb into bed and wait for your father to come up."

Alexandra's eyes widened a fraction but she didn't say anything. Laurel grabbed the brush, approached the girl and started taking down her pigtails. With the first stroke of the brush in her hair, Alexandra's posture relaxed. Her shoulders sagging as if she'd been holding the weight of the world on them.

Brushing the tangles from her hair, Laurel said, "Your mother must have had hair this color."

"She did." Alexandra stood a bit straighter. "There's a picture of her on the dresser."

Laurel turned her head and sure enough, a small photograph sat amongst the other gewgaws Alexandra had filling the surface. "She was very beautiful."

"Yeah. My pa said she was the purdiest thing he'd ever seen. When Grandpa bought this land and moved them all out here, my ma's family was already living here and pa seen her when they went to school." She yawned, her jaw cracking from the effort. "There wasn't no school house then, though. They just met out by that old tree in town on warm days and pa said she sat down right beside him and smiled at him. He said he was taken with her right then."

Laurel laid the brush down and gathered Alexandra's hair, separating it into three strands to braid it. "How old were they?"

Alexandra giggled and shook her head. "Pa said he was fourteen. I can't imagine wanting to marry someone at that age. I can't imagine wanting to marry anyone at all."

"Well, you'll change your mind about that soon enough, trust me."

When the braid was done, Laurel tied the end off with a ribbon and walked back to the bed, holding the blankets back. "Hop in."

Alexandra settled, burrowing into the covers. "My pa said all men want someone to take care of them."

Laurel nodded her head. "Most of them do."

The girl stared up at her for long minutes before sighing. "Even though I still don't like ya much, I think it might be okay for you to marry my pa. I don't need a new momma," she said, her eyes narrowing a fraction, "but my pa wants someone to take care of him when he needs it and it looks like tonight is one of those times he was talking about. If you were his wife, then you'd always be here for when he needed ya."

Laurel's eyes stung as she stared down at Alexandra. She wasn't sure the girl would ever like her but she'd more or less just given Laurel her blessing, so to speak, to marry her father. She smiled down at her, her heart melting for this stubborn little girl. "I'd very much like to marry your father, Alexandra, and I promise not to mother you too much. I probably won't be very good at it anyway seeing how I've never been a mother before."

Alexandra yawned up at her. "I'll show you how when you don't do something right."

She turned over in the bed, pulled the covers up to her ears and closed her eyes. Laurel sat there staring down at her until she heard footsteps in the hall. Standing, she peeked out the door and saw Holden carrying a bucket of water. He stopped and turned his head to her. "Is she ready for bed?"

Pulling Alexandra's door shut, she went to him, took the bucket and waited until he'd entered the room before following him in. "She's in bed. Will probably be asleep before you get undressed, if her yawning is any indication."

Holden's room was smaller than Alexandra's. It was sparsely furnished, too, with nothing more than a bed, which no one had bothered to make up, and a four-drawer dresser against one wall. The dresser drawers were open, clothes spilling out over the edges and a pile of them were in a heap on the floor.

Laurel raised one eyebrow at him before closing the door and setting the bucket down on the floor. She crossed the room to where he stood and started unbuttoning his shirt. "Judging the state of this room, Mr. Avery, I do believe you need a wife."

He grinned down at her. "Well, I just so happen to be looking for a one, if you're interested."

Tugging his shirt loose from the waistband of his pants, careful of his burned side, she smiled and cast a glance up at his face. "I might be."

He went so still, Laurel wasn't even sure he was breathing. She pushed his shirt over his shoulders, pulling it down his arms and it wasn't until the ruined material hit the floor that he moved. He cupped her face in his hands, holding her head up so she'd look at him. "Say it."

"Say what?" she whispered.

His mouth slanted into a crooked grin. "Say you'll marry me."

Laurel smiled and leaned in closer to him. "I'll marry you—if you can promise me you won't go running into any more burning buildings. I'm not sure my heart can handle that again."

He wasted no time in kissing her, pulling her to him and wrapping his arms around her as if he hadn't been burned. Laurel felt the floor pitch sideways and grabbed hold of his shoulders while returning his kiss. When he finally pulled back, they were both panting for breath.

"When?" he asked.

"When what?"

Holden leaned his forehead against her own, the smile on his face dazzling. "When can we get married?"

"There isn't a preacher in the house, that I know of, so not tonight." She stepped back, out of his arms, and reached for the waistband of his pants." She held his gaze as she unfastened his pants, pushing the material down over his lean hips. She cast a look down, his erection growing as she undressed him. When she had him bare from head to toe, she grabbed the water bucket, dug inside for the cloth and soap he'd tossed in and spent the next ten minutes washing every inch of him.

She sat him on the bed when he was clean, examined his burned side and was happy to see it hadn't blistered. It wasn't bad. Irritated mostly. Looking up at him, she said, "I need a horse." At his curious expression, she smiled. "Or one of your ranch hands to see me back to town."

"You can stay here for the night."

She raised an eyebrow at him. "That would be entirely inappropriate."

He reached for her, tugging at the buttons on the front of her dress. "We'll be married soon enough. We've nothing to hide."

Laurel giggled and stood to avoid his wandering hands. "Be that as it may, tongues will waggle if I stay the night. Not to mention, your daughter is in the next room. What will she think?"

He stood and Laurel made a point to keep her gaze on his face. He was still stark naked and seeing him in the altogether was distracting enough as it was. "There are four empty rooms in this house. It's also late. You can sleep in one of the other rooms if it'll make you feel better and I can have you back to town before a single person knows you didn't sleep in that miserable little room behind the school."

At the mention of the school, Laurel knew her position as the town's teacher was as good as gone. Married women weren't allowed to teach in most areas and she wasn't sure how laid-back a town like Willow Creek actually was.

"What is it?" Holden asked, reaching out to cup one hand along her jaw.

She sighed, her chest tightening. "I'll not be allowed to teach if I marry you."

"There's no reason you can't," he said. "And we'll cross that bridge when we get to it."

He slipped on a clean pair of trousers and showed her to the room at the end of the hall, lighting the lamps after entering. It was a large space, with windows gracing two walls, lace curtains hanging in billowy tufts of white froth to the floor. The bed was a four-poster, large enough to take up most of the room. There was an old rocker in one corner, a crocheted afghan hanging across the back and a wardrobe with mirrored glass on both doors. The floor was covered by a large rug and the room smelled faintly of perfume.

She turned to look at Holden. "Is this the room you shared with your wife?"

He nodded and walked farther into the room. "It's the biggest bedroom in the house." He stared across the space, a sad smile covering his face. "I moved down the hall a few months after she died. I didn't want to be in here alone." He turned to face her. The smile was gone but she could still see a lingering sadness in his eyes.

"Do you still miss her?"

"At times." He ran a hand through his hair. "I miss talking to her. She had an easy smile. Always found something to laugh about." He smiled again but it didn't reach his eyes. He met her gaze and sighed. "I'm done grieving for her. Have been for a long time. But I do miss having someone here. A man gets lonely after a while and ten years is a damn long time to be alone."

She crossed the room and wrapped her arms around his waist, mindful of the burn, and laid her head on his chest. Neither spoke. They just stood there, holding each other, comforting and being comforted in the stillness.

He kissed her on the top of the head after long minutes and pulled back enough to look at her face. "I love you."

"I love you, too."

He smiled and it reached his eyes, a glistening look of happiness that hadn't been there moments before. "As much as I'd like to crawl into that big bed and have my way with you, I'm not sure I'm up to it."

"I'm not letting you bed me again until we're properly married, Holden Avery, especially not with your daughter right down the hall."

He chuckled, gave her a quick kiss and let go of her. "I'll see you in the morning."

Laurel stared at the closed door when he left and sighed before taking in the room again. It was lovely, decorated by his wife, she was sure, and she wondered if she'd done the right thing, saying she'd marry him. The fluttering in her chest told her she had but that stubborn part of her brain that said he'd only betray her later wouldn't shut up.

She turned down the bed sheets and removed her clothing, leaving her chemise on, and decided to worry about things tomorrow. She'd had too much happen in too short a time and truth be told, she was exhausted.

CHAPTER 12

THE RIDE back into town was made in the predawn twilight and as much as Laurel enjoyed the quiet ride with Holden on his black stallion, her nerves were a bit rattled.

She couldn't help but fear someone would see them. She'd heard enough gossip in this small community to know tongues would be wagging if they were seen.

Luckily, they made it to the school without seeing another living soul and Holden helped her to the ground, gave her a toe-curling kiss and left before anyone saw him.

She rounded the building and stopped short when she looked at the door to her room. A bouquet of flowers lay on her stoop, a bright pink ribbon holding them together and her mind registered the fact she'd seen them before. Ethan had been holding them only yesterday as they quarreled in front of the mercantile. Finding them on her stoop, now, infuriated her.

Walking up the steps, she kicked the flowers to one side, opened the door and hoped she didn't find any surprises inside. Ethan wasn't there, thank goodness, and nothing looked out of place.

She busied herself with washing, changing into a clean dress and walked through the door that led to the school room. Standing at the front of the room, she inhaled the scent of chalk and musty books. She'd miss this when she had to give it up. She loved teaching and as much as she loved Holden, a part of her didn't want to give up something she'd worked so hard to attain. She'd made sacrifices and hard choices to get her degree and letting it go would be bittersweet.

HOLDEN WAITED PATIENTLY until Mrs. Jenkins unlocked the door to the mercantile, offering her a greeting as she smiled up at him.

"You're out and about awfully early."

"I have a lot to do today," he said, waiting until she shut the door before walking to the counter. "Do you still have that case of jewelry?"

She raised one eyebrow at him, giving him a bemused grin before nodding her head and reaching for the small box she kept hidden. She laid it on the counter and opened the lid. "Are you looking for something specific?"

He looked into the box, eyeing the cluster of pieces and nodded. "A ring. Gold if you have it."

Mrs. Jenkins fingered the necklaces and brooches in the box to find a buried treasure of rings that lay in the bottom. She pulled them out, laid them on the lid of the box and smiled. "This is all I have left. A gentleman was in here just yesterday and bought the nicest one. It was the only real gold I had, even though it wasn't anything fancy. Just a simple gold band, really."

Holden looked up. "Anyone we know?"

She shook her head. "No. I've never seen him before. He looked to have a bit of money on him, if you could judge such a thing by a man's clothing. He was wearing a suit and he talked a bit fancy, too."

Ethan. Holden knew that's who bought the ring without being

told and he knew the reason he had. Resentment and just plain jealousy caused his breath to catch. Was Ethan going to propose to Laurel... again? Try and court her?

Even though Laurel said she'd marry him, he couldn't rest easy until she'd said, "I do." She had a history with Ethan, she'd loved the man at one time and even though she claimed to no longer hold any affection for the man, Holden wasn't going to waste time waiting for Ethan to make a move.

He thanked Mrs. Jenkins and left the store, walking at a fast clip to Morgan's house and pounded on the door until his brother opened it. "I have to go to Missoula. Keep an eye on Laurel while I'm gone."

Morgan raised one eyebrow. "Good morning to you too," he said. "What's going on in Missoula?"

Holden didn't have time, or the inclination, to get into it. "Just something I have to do. Have you seen Ethan Dearborn around town?"

Morgan nodded. "Yeah. He was having breakfast in the hotel when I passed by there. Why?"

"Don't let him get near Laurel until I get back." He turned, hurried down the front porch steps and turned back before exiting the gate. "I should be back by nightfall but have Percy send one of the men over at the livery stable out to the ranch and let them know where I've gone."

He crossed the street, gathered his horse and was riding away from Willow Creek before it dawned on him that he hadn't even told Laurel his plans. He didn't want to waste the time going back to tell her and leaned over his horse's back, urging him into a faster run. He was losing time and with Ethan still in town, he had precious little of it left to make things happen.

IT WAS near noon when Abigail walked into the school house

from the entrance that led to Laurel's room. Her new friend smiled at her as she laid a basket on the edge of Laurel's desk.

"I knocked but you never answered so I let myself in." She uncovered the basket, pulling a plate of sandwiches out and laid them on the desk. "I thought we could have lunch together, unless you've already eaten."

Laurel smiled and laid her pencil down. "I'm starved, actually. I missed breakfast."

Abigail grinned and pulled a chair up beside the desk. "So I've heard."

Laurel's heart skipped a beat and Abigail laughed while shaking her head. "Morgan saw you riding in with Holden this morning but your secret is safe with me." She blushed, an apologetic look on her face. "In all the excitement last night, I'm ashamed to say we just plain forgot about you. I hope you can forgive us."

Laurel smiled, reassuring her. "It's fine. I wouldn't have wanted to leave before I knew Holden was all right and had time to talk to him, anyway."

"He was okay, then?"

"For the most part," Laurel told her. "He had a burn on his side but it wasn't bad, thankfully."

They had their sandwiches, and discussed the fire in Holden's barn the day before and as much as remembering still scared her to think what could have happened, she let Abigail talk.

"I just find it strange anyone would be so careless," she was saying. "I know a few of the ranch hands smoke but none of them would be so stupid as to do so in the barn. It just makes no sense, really."

Laurel hadn't given much thought to what may have caused the fire but now that Abigail brought it up, she could think of nothing else. It was hard to tell what started it, especially seeing how nothing had been left but a smoldering pile of charred wood but an uneasy feeling churned in her gut. She wondered if Ethan would be so devious as to start a fire and knew he was before the thought fully formed.

She ignored the notion. They finished their lunch, washed it down with a pot a tea and Abigail was repacking her basket when Laurel noticed her friend in no hurry to leave. Abigail sat back down after the remains of their lunch had been put away and Laurel watched her, curious as to why she was still lingering. Not that she minded, it just seemed odd. Abigail had a family, after all. "How are Morgan and Elizabeth?"

"They're fine. Morgan was putting Elizabeth down for a nap when I left."

Laurel nodded her head and waited. Abigail seemed to take interest in the school room, her head turning in all directions to take everything in. It wasn't until she saw Abigail look at the small watch pin, which hung from a chain around her neck, that she grew suspicious. "Are you waiting for something, Abigail?"

Her friend's eyes widened just a fraction. "What would I be waiting for?"

"I don't know," Laurel said, smiling. "You just look... well, settled in. I'm sure you have better things to do than to sit with me while I go over lesson plans."

Abigail laughed nervously and stood, grabbed her basket and said, "You're right. I do have things to do today. Thanks for lunch!"

She hurried across the room, leaving through the front door of the school and was gone in seconds. Laurel sat staring at the door for long moments before laughing quietly to herself and resuming her lesson plans. Not five minutes later, Morgan Avery walked through the door. Laurel knew something was up, then.

He smiled as he crossed the room, tipping his hat to her before grabbing the chair his wife had just vacated, turning it to sit astraddle the seat. "Afternoon," he said, smiling.

Laurel nodded her head in his direction. "Morgan. What can I do for you?"

"Nothing. I just thought we could have a talk." He grinned, the smile looking a bit forced. "If Holden has his way, we'll be related soon, so I thought we could get to know each other better."

Her face heated at that. Had Holden told his brother she'd said yes to his marriage proposal? She hadn't told Abigail because the idea was still so new. Besides, no date had been set, no plans made, so it all seems a bit premature at this point. "Does your brother usually get his way?" she asked, for lack of anything else to say.

Morgan chuckled. "He's an Avery. We always get what we want."

Laurel smiled at that. Those Averys were also very sure of themselves. "It won't hurt one of you to not get his way."

A blinding smile met her gaze. "Probably not but we're not willing to find out how it'd feel not to." He shifted on his seat, repositioned his hat and laid his forearms over the back of his chair. "And Holden's waited a lot longer than we have to find someone. He's always known he was a family man. Even when we were younger, all he really wanted was a wife, kids and that ranch. The rest of us were content to just visit the saloons and live one day at a time. Holden's always been a bit different and he's not been interested in anyone since Maggie died. Not seriously, anyway." He smiled at her again. "Well, until you came along." He met her gaze and held it. "He loves you, Laurel. He'll make a good husband for you."

The words, I know, were on the tip of her tongue but Laurel held them back. For the same reason she hadn't told Abigail about their impending marriage, she kept the knowledge from Morgan. She offered him a smile in response and movement behind him caught her attention. Looking to the front door, her heart skipped a beat. "Ethan? What are you doing here?"

Morgan stood and turned toward the door, crossing his arms over his chest. Laurel knew by his posture he'd been waiting for this. She assumed it's also why she'd had constant company since

Holden had dropped her off at the school. He was having her...babysat like an infant. Her temper flared but she let it go and stood.

Ethan was again dressed in a suit, dark gray this time. His shoes had a shine on them she could see from across the room. He was also carrying another bouquet of flowers. He removed his hat, tipped his head in her direction and said, "Good afternoon, Laurel." His gaze shifted to Morgan. "Marshal."

He entered the room fully, crossed the space between them and stuck his hand out, offering her the flowers. "These are for you, my love."

The smile on his face was sickly sweet and Laurel blew out a breath of frustration. As much as she didn't want the flowers, she reached out and took them anyway, laying them on her desk. If accepting them was what it would take to make him go away, then so be it. "Thank you."

He straightened the lapels of his jacket, casting a quick glance to Morgan before returning his attention back to her. "I came to ask you to lunch. I had them set a special table for us over at the hotel."

Laurel's stomach was in knots by the time he stopped talking. He was up to something. She knew him too well not to know. "I've already had lunch."

"Oh." He looked disappointed but brightened a moment later. "Supper then. I can come back," he pulled a watch from his pocket, the gleaming gold chain winking as the sun shining in through the window caught it, "say, around four."

She opened her mouth to respond but Morgan spoke before she had a chance. "She's already accepted an invitation to supper at my house this evening."

Morgan didn't so much as glance her way but his lie was delivered as smooth as any she'd heard. She was amused and grateful. "That's right," she said. "I already have plans."

Ethan smiled and tipped his head toward her. "Some other

time, then." Nodding to Morgan, he turned without another word.

When he was out of sight, Laurel let go of the breath she'd been holding and sank back down into her seat. Morgan turned to look at her and frowned. "Is he always so persistent?"

Laurel laughed. "Most of the time, yes." She didn't add that he had a reason to be. That he would inherit a fortune from her father if—and when—he married her. Whatever business deal her father and Ethan had, it must have been profitable for Ethan to chase her across several territories and linger once he found her.

Morgan stayed for another half hour, talking about nothing really but the moment he left, Laurel breathed a sigh of relief. Knowing her constant stream of visitors were just there to help fend off Ethan only served as a reminder that he was there and the sooner she could forget about him, the better off she was.

She secured the front door of the school so no one could get in from outside and walked to her little room in the back and did the same. She looked around the small space she'd been calling home and sighed.

The little room wasn't much but it was hers and giving it up would be hard. She'd given up so much to find the position, to live her dream of teaching, and she'd run away from home to be able to have it. Now, she was giving it up to marry a man who just wouldn't take no for an answer.

"Maybe I'm making a mistake," she said to no one. She sat on the edge of her bed, her mind a jumble of what ifs.

If she married Holden, she'd be sacrificing everything she'd ever wanted. But not marrying him meant giving up the one thing she craved. A family. Someone who loved her. A place to call home.

Doubts were creeping in and the guilt that followed caused her heart to ache. She hadn't lied when she told Holden she loved him.

She did, but what if it didn't work? What if all the fears she had became a reality? If Holden grew tired of her, would he stray? Find a mistress to give him what he was no longer willing to take from her?

Misery settled like a stone in her stomach and she felt sick, queasiness churning in her belly. She gulped in air, closed her eyes and willed the feeling away. "Everything will be fine," she told herself. Opening her eyes, she sighed. "It has to be."

IT WAS after midnight when Holden rode back into town. He didn't think he'd ever been as saddle-sore or weary in his life. He'd had to stop nearly two hours ago to rest the horse. The stallion was sturdy and good for long distances but even the best horse couldn't keep walking but so long.

The town was quiet when they lumbered through the street. The noise from the saloon subdued. No one lingered on the boardwalk and other than the lamplights shining from the windows of the saloon, the town was dark.

He wanted to see Laurel but knew she had classes come sunup. Disturbing her at this hour of night would be unseemly but he couldn't wait. He guided his horse around the side of the school and stopped, climbed wearily from his horse and unhooked the parcels tied to his saddlebags.

There weren't any lights coming from the one small window to her room and trying the door, he found it bolted from the inside. He sighed, ran a weary hand over his face and knocked. He heard the bedsprings squeak then, moments later, her voice.

"Who's there?"

"Holden."

She opened the door, squinting in the darkness to see him. "What's wrong?"

"Nothing," he said, smiling down at her. Her hair was mussed, her pristine white gown swallowing the curves he knew she had and just seeing her lifted his spirits.

Grabbing his arm, she pulled him inside the room and shut the door behind him. "Where have you been all day? Morgan said you had to go to Missoula."

He nodded. "I had a few things to take care of that wouldn't wait." He held out the packages to her, waiting for her to take them. "That's for you," he said. "And the preacher will be here on Sunday if you still have a mind to marry me." He held his breath, hoping she hadn't changed her mind.

She smiled at him and laid the packages on the end of the bed. "I'll probably live to regret it, but yes, I still plan on marrying you."

Relief flooded his system and he wrapped her in his arms, laid his chin on her head and just stood there holding her.

"What's in the packages?" she asked.

He smiled and kissed the top of her head. "You'll see when you open them." Pulling away from her, he cupped her cheek in one hand. "As much as it kills me to leave, I have to go. Alex is probably beside herself since I didn't go home after dropping you off." He kissed her, briefly, and turned to the door. "I'll see you tomorrow."

Once outside, he waited until he heard her bolt the door again before crossing the space to his horse. He climbed into the saddle, let out a weary sigh and reined the horse toward home. Once he'd left the town proper, he raised his arm, stuck his hand into his coat pocket and smiled when his fingers grazed the small package stowed there. He'd spent a good chunk of his savings on it but come spring, when the new colts were born, he'd make the money back and then some. Besides, it wasn't everyday one found a woman like Laurel and to him, seeing her happy was worth every penny he had.

Despite the fact she had classes in the morning, the packages Holden dropped off were too intriguing to not open. Laurel lit a lamp and sat down on the bed, pulling the string holding the smallest wrapped parcel open. Yards of snow-white lace spilled from the brown wrapping. She lifted it, took in the detail in the design and was grinning in an instant.

She laid the lace aside, reached for the remaining package, a large bundle tied with two separate strings and wasted no time unwrapping the treasure. What she found lying inside took her breath.

Standing, she grabbed the dress at the shoulders and held it up, a billow of white satin and lace flowing to the floor. Her eyes burned as she looked at it. Holden had gone all the way to Missoula to buy her a dress?

Tears clouded her eyes at the thought. She hadn't even considered what she'd wear to marry him, the idea was still so fresh on her mind, but he'd taken the burden away from her. He'd delivered a white wedding gown Queen Victoria herself would envy.

She laughed suddenly, hugging the dress to her and gazing down at the bed where she'd laid the yard of lace. She noticed something in the bottom of the package the dress had come from and reached for it, more laughter bubbling forth when she picked up the small, silk slippers tucked into the folds of the wrapping. He'd thought of everything.

Wiping her face dry, she stored the dress, the slippers and the lace in the wardrobe, folded the wrapping paper and put it away, along with the twine and extinguished the lamp. She lay staring at the ceiling, knowing she'd never be able to sleep. By weeks end she'd be married. To a man too wonderful to be true.

CHAPTER 13

THE FOLLOWING SUNDAY MORNING, the sky was laden with slate-gray clouds and a chill wind blew in from the mountains. Laurel stood in the small room behind the school house with nervous butterflies swimming in her stomach.

The week had passed in a blur of events that had Laurel ready to just throw up her hands, hop on the first stagecoach out of town, and get as far away as she could. Between the endless stream of visits from Ethan—who seemed in no short supply of gifts, his idea of courting her, she supposed—she was at her wits end. Ethan's visits put her on edge especially after the local gossip about her impending marriage to Holden reached him. Ethan tried to persuade her to marry him, going so far as to produce a ring, and resorted to threats when she refused.

A classroom full of rowdy children didn't help matters either. Not to mention, Alexandra, the child she would soon call a daughter, had become withdrawn. She sat in class with her head down, never spoke unless she was asked a specific question and Laurel was worried on so many levels, the stress was sure to kill her at any moment. Holden hadn't been able to calm her fears any either. All the man ever said was, "It'll all be fine. Just wait and see."

She wished she had an ounce of his confidence. The closer to Sunday it drew, the stronger the sense of foreboding grew. Something was going to stop this wedding. Laurel just knew it.

"Hold still," Abigail said, grabbing Laurel's shoulder and turning her the way she needed her to stand. "I only have a few more stitches and you'll be done."

Laurel stopped fidgeting and stared out the window. Emmaline and Abigail had shown up right after breakfast to do the last minute alterations to her dress. They'd rearranged the school house the day before, removing the desks and lining the benches up for everyone to sit at since there wasn't a church, or a building large enough to hold everyone who may show up, in Willow Creek. Fall flowers and ribbons decorated the room and Holden had met the circuit preacher and tucked him away in the hotel to await the wedding. Everything was in place, the clock ticking off the minutes and in less than an hour, she'd be Laurel Avery, wife to Holden and new mother to Alexandra.

She turned her head when she heard the sound of dragging feet and smiled when Alexandra poked her head in the door. She was wearing a dress the color of a summer sky. The pale blue material was trimmed in lace and small delicate flowers had been woven into her blond hair which fell in curly waves down her back. "You look beautiful, Alexandra."

The girl's cheeks turned pink but she wouldn't meet her gaze. She watched Abigail, looked around the small room and sighed heavily.

"Is there anything wrong?" Laurel asked.

Alexandra shrugged one shoulder.

Abigail stepped around her, smiling, drawing her attention away from Alexandra. "There. All done." She beamed up at her, her eyes dancing with mirth. "I don't think I've ever seen a lovelier bride."

Laurel thanked her and waited until Abigail had put all her sewing notions away before turning to face Alexandra. She was still by the door looking at anything but her. "Could I have a word with Alexandra?" Laurel said, never taking her eyes off the girl. "Alone, please."

Abigail and Emmaline said nothing. Just grabbed their things and left the room, pulling the door shut behind them.

"Would you like to sit down?"

Alexandra sighed again and shook her head.

Laurel crossed the room and stooped down to be eye level with her. "What is it?"

It took Alexandra a few moments but she finally raised her head and met her gaze. Her eyes were glassy with unshed tears. "I changed my mind," she said. "I don't want you to marry my pa."

She'd been expecting something, but this wasn't it. Laurel took a moment to collect her thoughts before nodding her head. "All right." She tried to smile, failed at the attempt. "Will you at least tell me why?"

The tears shimmering in Alexandra's eyes slipped past her lashes and Laurel reached up to brush them away. The girl sucked in a breath and let it out before sniffling. "If my pa marries you, he may not love me as much anymore."

"Oh, Alexandra." Laurel's heart went out to the girl, despite their rocky relationship. She smiled and held her arms out, hoping Alexandra would accept her offer. It took a few moments but she reluctantly accepted and stepped into Laurel's embrace.

"Your daddy loves you more than anything in this world," she said. "Even me. Nothing will ever change that. The love he has for you is different from everyone else. What we feel for a friend or a parent is different than a child or a wife or husband. You'll always be first in his heart. Always."

Alexandra sniffled again and raised her head. "You're not just saying that?"

Laurel smiled, her own eyes burning. "No, I'm not just saying that." She pushed Alexandra's hair across her shoulder. "If you feel this strongly about it though, maybe you should talk to your pa and tell him. I'm sure he'll understand."

The look on Alexandra's face said she'd rather do anything else in the world than say any such thing to Holden. She sighed, scrubbed a hand across her nose and met her gaze. "No. He wants you to marry him and I already said it was okay. He'll not be happy if I tell him I've changed my mind. Not today." She shook her head. "He was smiling this morning bigger than I've seen in a while. It wouldn't be fair to make him call off the wedding."

Laurel's breath whooshed out in relief. She smiled and stood, stretching out her back when she straightened. "Everything will work out fine, Alex. Just wait and see."

Alex's eyes widened as she looked up at Laurel. "You called me Alex."

"That I did." Laurel smiled down at her again. "My wedding gift to you. I'll not force anyone to call you Alexandra if you prefer to be called Alex."

The girl's face lit up. "Does that mean you're not going to make me wear dresses after you and pa get married?"

Laurel laughed. "Not on your life. You'll grow to be a proper young lady if it kills me."

They stood staring at each other before Laurel smiled. "I do have a favor to ask of you though. And I'd be honored if you'd accept."

Alex looked up, a curious look in her eyes. "What kind of favor?"

Laurel smiled and held out one hand. "Something that will please your pa, I'm sure."

THEY ENTERED the school from the front. Inside the building, nearly everyone from town waited. There were faces looking back at Laurel that she'd never seen before and she knew she was all but glowing when she looked across the room to where Holden stood. He looked handsome in his black suit jacket. He'd even had his hair trimmed and much to her shock, he'd shaved. She wasn't sure the last time she'd seen him clean shaven.

His gaze drank her in before it shifted to Alex. The girl was beaming at her father, the smile causing her eyes to sparkle. Alex looked up at Laurel, held out her hand and said, "Let's go get you married to my pa."

Alexandra walked Laurel down the makeshift isle to the front of the room, stopping once they reached Holden and the preacher. She smiled at her father, raised Laurel's hand before grabbing Holden's and laid their hands palm to palm. "I give this woman to you to wife."

A light chorus of laughter filled the small school room. Laurel winked at the girl as she turned and took a seat with Abigail and Morgan. Turning to face Holden, the butterflies in her stomach quivered before coming to a complete stop.

The preacher was a burly man with a shock of white hair and a full beard streaked with red. The end of his bulbous nose was red and his voice, deep and booming, filled the room as he said, "We are gathered here today..."

Laurel couldn't take her eyes off Holden. He still held her hand, his handsome face the only thing she saw, and her heart pounded so hard in her chest she wondered if everyone gathered could hear it.

She'd slept little the night before, the sense of impending doom following her through the night and Alexandra showing up and confessing she didn't want the marriage to take place caused the feelings to grow. The preacher asked if anyone had just cause for them not to be lawfully joined, to speak now or forever hold their peace, and a hush rushed over the waiting crowd.

Holden smiled at her, his hand tightening in hers and Laurel didn't take a breath until the preacher started talking again.

Holden said, "I do," at the appropriate time and as Laurel was asked, she inhaled a breath to ensure her voice didn't squeak. When she said, "I do," in return, the front door slammed open, hitting the wall and causing several shrieks of fright.

Ethan stood framed in the sunlight, the sneer on his face condescending. "I object," he said, catching her gaze. "This wedding is a farce."

Laurel felt dizzy and if the room hadn't been filled with people, she was sure to have fainted. She gaped at Ethan a full minute before raged filled her.

Holden's hand tightened in hers, his voice a harsh whisper when he said, "Can I kill him?"

It took her longer than it should have to answer. "N-n-no. I've already watched you run into a burning building. I know my heart couldn't take seeing you hang."

Ethan, proud of himself, if the smile on his face was any indication, waited by the door, looking smug and satisfied. He tilted his head to one side, the sneer growing. "I do believe your father would object to this wedding as well."

Laurel turned to face Ethan, felt the gaze of almost everyone in the room and she wasn't sure what was more embarrassing. Having her wedding interrupted or the scene that caused it. "My father's not here," she said. "Besides, I'm a grown woman. I don't need his permission."

Movement behind Ethan's back caused Laurel to still, a shadowy form filling the doorway. A man stepped into the room, his cane hitting the wooden floor in crisp, hard taps. Her eyes widened. "Father?"

Her father looked none too pleased, the scowl on his face showing his displeasure. Laurel felt her eyes burn with tears. She knew that impending doom she'd felt for days wasn't just a case of nerves now. She should have left town the minute Ethan showed up, running and not stopping until she was clean across the ocean.

She blew out a breath, cast a sad glance to Alexandra and turned to face Holden. "I'm sorry, Holden."

"For what?" he asked.

"My father always gets his way. He'll never allow this."

A muscle ticked in Holden's jaw, his eyes narrowing. "Do you want to marry me?" The question was asked in a soft whisper.

She nodded. "Yes."

"Then you will." He let go of her hand and started for the door, a few gasps filling the silence. Morgan and Colt stepped out into the isle, following Holden, and Laurel thought for sure her weak knees would give out.

Holden spoke with her father, throwing a scornful look at Ethan and when all five men left the school, Laurel let go of the breath she'd been holding.

Abigail took her by one elbow, ushered her to the bench she'd vacated and told her to sit.

"The whole day is ruined," Laurel said. "I should have left when I had a chance."

"You don't mean that." Abigail squatted down in front of her. "Everything will be fine. You'll see."

Laurel wasn't so sure about that. She'd been truthful when she said her father always got his way. Walter Montgomery was a man used to having everything he wanted and if he wanted her to marry Ethan, she'd marry him. Assuming they caught her first. It's why she'd ran in the first place.

Murmurs and soft whispers filled the room and long minutes of waiting caused those butterflies Laurel had finally gotten rid of to return. She chewed her bottom lip, stared at the flowers in her hand, the petals wilting along with her spirits and half an hour later, a hushed silence filled the air. Laurel turned her head to the door, saw Holden walk back in, her father at his side, and rose to her feet.

Her father smiled when he stepped in front of her, reaching

out to take her hand. "This the man you want?" he asked, his voice gruff.

Laurel blinked and nodded her head. "Yes, sir."

He nodded his head once and turned to look at Holden. "Well, get on with it then. I'm not getting any younger."

Walter Montgomery shouldered his way onto a bench on the front row, sat ram-rod straight and placed both hands on the top of his cane. The look in his eye was challenging and Laurel wasn't sure why he'd changed his mind, nor did she care.

They took their places in front of the preacher again and Laurel glanced back at the door. All three of Holden's brothers stood framed in sunlight, their arms crossed over their chest. She wasn't sure where Ethan had gone but one thing was for sure. He wasn't getting back in that school house.

"What happened?" she whispered.

Holden grinned at her. "Your father is a businessman. I presented him with an offer he couldn't refuse. Apparently the government is in need of good, sturdy horses and your father has agreed to help me negotiate a contract. This marriage is going to make us all quite wealthy and a man like your father isn't a fool."

The preacher started the ceremony again. Laurel barely heard a word he said but managed to say her vows without losing her breath. When the preacher asked for the ring, her hand shook as she held it out, her gaze riveted to the gold band Holden placed on her finger. Her pulse leaped as the light caught the small jewels inlaid with the gold. Small diamonds and rubies winked in the sunlight coming from the window.

When the preacher presented them as man and wife, the noise inside that small building nearly lifted the rafters. Laurel laughed, waited for a kiss from her husband, and wasn't sure she could have been any happier.

EPILOGUE

ONE YEAR LATER

HOLDEN SIGNED FOR THE TRANSFER, tipped his hat at the men waiting and waved them off as they started herding the horses toward the main road. He turned back toward the house, nearly running to reach the porch and took the steps two at a time.

Everyone was still in the parlor, expectant looks on their faces. A small shake of Morgan's head, and Holden heaved a sigh. He hadn't missed it.

He stood in the doorway, the urge to pace the room strong as shadows started creeping into the room. He heard Alex, her voice pitched low as she entertained Elizabeth, Morgan and Abigail's daughter. He glanced to Sarah, a smile on her face as she played with her infant daughter, Catherine, Colt watching on as he held Emma.

The tension drained from his shoulders as he turned his gaze to Tristan and Emmaline. His brother was lifting his pregnant wife's feet, forcing them onto a stool, and the scowl Emmaline shot him never reached her eyes.

His entire family had gathered, all of them clustered together in the parlor and his father lifted his head when a shrill cry filled the house. James stood, and looked toward Holden. "Better get on up there, boy. They don't scream like that for nothing."

Holden turned, fairly raced up the stairs, and met Abigail as she walked out into the hall. She was smiling, tears clinging to her lashes and she laid one hand to his arm before motioning inside the room with a tilt of her head. "Go on in."

He waited until she left the hall before looking into the room. Laurel was pale, dark shadows lay under her eyes like bruises, but the smile on her face couldn't be missed. She glanced up at him, her smile widening before she looked at the squirming bundle in her arms.

"Come meet your son, Holden."

He entered the room, his heart slamming against his ribcage as he approached the bed. His knees gave out when he reached it and he sank into the mattress, his gaze riveted to the pink, wriggling baby. His son. He laughed, reached over to run his hand lightly atop his head, mussing the dark tufts of downy curls. "He's perfect." He cleared his throat, dislodging the lump forming, and looked up. "You're okay?"

Laurel nodded her head. "I've never felt more alive."

Alex burst into the room, her eyes wide. "You're not gonna die?"

Laurel laughed. "Not for a very long time." She held her arm out, motioning Alex closer. "Come say hello to your brother."

Holden stood, allowing Alex to join Laurel and watched his family, huddled in the blankets of his bed. His brothers and sisters-in-law crowded outside the door, all their faces lit with smiles.

He caught Laurel's gaze, felt his heart soar when she whispered, "I love you," and the fear he'd been secretly holding on to for the last nine months evaporated in an instant. She was strong, his wife. She wouldn't leave him. She wouldn't die. He wouldn't let her even if she tried.

Dear Reader,

The Avery men are the backbone of Willow Creek but the towns-folk are what make it the quaint little community it is. The rest of the series will feature people we've already met in the first four books and a few we haven't.

The next book, His Brother's Wife, features characters that were briefly mentioned in book one. Remember when Morgan and Abigail's 'honeymoon' was interrupted by a young boy, Jesse, who had run all the way to town because his mother had passed away? Well, this book will feature him and his older brother, Rafe. To find out what their story is all about, flip the page for a sneak-peek.

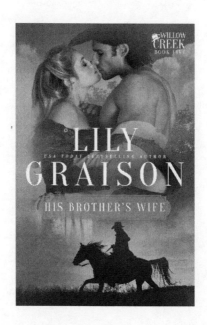

Chapter One

He was going to skin that boy alive.

Rafe bit his tongue to keep from shouting and crossed the yard to the barn, his heated gaze on Jesse. Stopping by the fence, he adjusted his hat and propped his foot on the bottom rung. And waited. He hid a smile when Jesse stopped, turned to face him and yelled, "What?"

Rafe propped his arms on his raised knee. "Just wondering where the hell you think you're going. We've got things to do around here, if you haven't noticed."

Jesse rolled his eyes and cinched the mule before leading him to the wagon. "I got places to be today."

"Like?"

"Like none of your damn business."

Straightening, Rafe raised an eyebrow at him. "You aren't too big for me to take a belt to your hide."

Jesse scoffed. "Try it."

"Don't tempt me." The rebellious look on his brother's face darkened, the freckles splattered across Jesse's cheeks and nose the same color as the thick thatch of red hair on his head. In the ten years he'd been gone, the kid had grown almost as tall as he was. His attitude had too. He lowered his leg to the ground and tried to keep the irritation out of his voice. "Where are you going, Jesse?"

"Town."

"What for?" Jesse mumbled something under his breath, his face growing brighter red before he turned his back to him. His movements were jerky, his shoulders held rigid. "We don't need anything from town that can't wait and that hole in the barn roof isn't going to fix itself. Unhitch that mule and go grab that bucket of nails out by the work shed." Rafe walked off, hoping Jesse would just do as told for once.

A glance over his shoulder and he bit his tongue, trying to rein in his temper. Jesse was still hitching up the mule. Rafe stopped, turned to look at him again, and had to remind himself that killing a man, even your own kin, was illegal. If the boy didn't already hate him with a passion he'd be tempted to take a belt to his backside just as he'd threatened to do.

He watched him finish hitching the mule, his lips bloodless from pinching them together. The silence stretched until Rafe thought he could touch it. "Jesse, what did I say?"

"I don't really give a damn what you said. Fix the barn yourself. I have things to do."

That was it. The last straw. Rafe closed the distance between them at a fast clip, his booted feet hitting the ground in loud pops. "And what would that be?"

Jesse swallowed and licked his lips. His face went a funny shade of white before he whispered, "I ordered me a wife."

It took Rafe a full minute before what Jesse said registered. He stared down at him, letting the words rattle around in his head before he blinked and focused his eyes. "You want to run that by me one more time?"

Jesse flicked a quick look at him before lowering his head. "I ordered me a wife." He swallowed, his throat moving as he did before he lifted his head, his eyes flashing. "And don't go yelling at me for it either cause it ain't going to do you no good."

He ordered a wife? Rafe tried to wrap his head around the statement but as much as he tried, it just didn't make sense. Jesse wasn't old enough to marry. He was just a kid but there he stood, head held high, shoulders back and looking as sure as any man about to make the biggest mistake of their life.

He bit his tongue to keep from shouting what a little fool he was, adjusting his hat instead, and propped his foot on the wagon wheel to give himself more time to collect his thoughts. When he knew he could speak without yelling, he opened his mouth. Nothing came out.

Jesse's face turned a light shade of pink before the look in his eyes turned murderous. "Just get to the yelling part, Rafe. I've got places to be and you're wasting my time!"

Rafe flinched. Jesse's high pitched voice grated on his nerves most days, more so when he yelled. The urge to bend the boy over his knee was strong but he refused to treat Jesse like a child even though, in his eyes, the kid would always be his little brother.

When he left home ten years ago, the kid has been docile and sweet natured. That wasn't the case now. Since the day he'd returned six months ago, Jesse had fought him at every turn. Everything he said turned into a battle of wills and he was at his whit's end trying to figure out where he'd gone wrong. His pa would have whipped that boy bloody for talking to him the way he did.

Why he was the lucky recipient of his anger was a mystery he'd never figure out.

Crossing his arms over his chest, he narrowed his eyes and

pinned Jesse with a glare of his own. "I heard that part, little brother. What I want to know is why?"

The mutinous glare Jesse shot him should have scorched the skin right off of him. "Stop calling me little! I'm fifteen years old."

"Fourteen. You have nine whole months before you'll be fifteen."

"So?"

"So… you're too young to get married." The fire in Jesse's eyes matched the temper the boy had developed over the years. "And you are little." Rafe grinned. "My little brother."

Jesse's face turned red again, his fingers curling into his hands to make fists. "I'm tired of everyone in this town calling me your little brother. I'm a man. Have been since pa died and you were off doing God only knows what. It's about time people saw me as a man, so, I ordered me a wife."

Rafe leaned his head to one side. "And what do you plan on doing with her?"

"Doing with her?" Jesse stared at him wide-eyed. "What do you think I'm going to do with her? I'll make her clean the house and cook my meals. Wash clothes and make sure my socks don't have no holes in them."

"And?" Rafe prompted.

"And what?"

Rafe laughed. The boy didn't have the first clue what he was getting himself in to. "How old is this wife you ordered?"

Jesse shrugged his shoulder. "I don't know."

"You don't know?" Rafe raised an eyebrow at him. "What does she look like?" Another shoulder shrug was all the answer he got. "You do realize most of those mail-order brides are plain and dowdy looking spinsters that no other man would marry, right?"

"What difference does it make? I didn't order her to look at."

It was obvious his brother didn't have the first clue what a wife was for. Sure those other things were nice but a man didn't take a woman to wife just to make a house servant out of her. He wanted a nice warm body to keep him warm at night. A sweet smelling little thing to make the hard days seem a little less rough. Someone to bear his children.

Rafe grinned and slapped Jesse on the shoulder. "You're right, Jesse. If your wife is here to cook and clean for you, and darn your socks, what difference does it make how old she is or what she looks like. Tell you what. When she gets here, I'll let you have the big room at the top of the stairs. We can't have your bride sleeping in that tiny room of yours, now can we?"

Jesse's face went a funny shade of white and he raised his hand, scratching the side of his neck. "Why do I need Ma and Pa's old room?"

"For you and your new bride."

When Jesse spoke again, it was a tiny sound that squeaked. "You mean I have to sleep in the same room with her?"

Rafe bit his lip to keep from laughing again. "That's what men do when they take a wife."

"But there ain't but one bed in there."

"Then you'll have to share."

Jesse swallowed, his throat moving with the small action before the boy turned and looked back out over the field. "It'll be okay if she takes that room by herself. I'm comfortable where I am."

The sun was overhead and Rafe felt his stomach give a painful twist. It was past lunch. He looked toward Jesse, seeing his red-tinted face, and the defiance in his eyes, and knew regardless of what he said, the kid would fight him every step of the way.

Bracing himself for the outburst, Rafe nodded toward the house. "Best go on in there and write that bride of yours a letter and tell her you've changed your mind. You're not old enough for a wife, Jesse. You don't even know what a man wants one for."

He turned to the barn, and the gaping hole in the roof he had to fix, and motioned to the mule. "When you get finished with that, come put the mule away and help me with the roof." He'd taken four steps when Jesse threw his hat at him, hitting him in the back.

"Don't tell me what to do, Rafe! I'm through taking orders from you. Besides, I can't send no letter. She'll be here today."

Rafe turned to face his brother. "What do you mean she'll be here today?"

Jesse raised his chin a notch. "I sent away for her months ago. She's supposed to be on the stagecoach today. That's why I was hitching up the wagon. I'm going in to town to pick her up and see if that preacher is still over at the hotel."

The mule was hitched to the wagon and Rafe stared at it for long moments before looking back at Jesse. The kid was serious. He could tell by the look in his eyes. "Jesse, you can't marry some strange woman regardless of what you think. You're too young. There isn't a preacher this side of the Mississippi that would do it."

"We'll see about that." Picking up his hat, Jesse brushed it off and put it back on his head, shielding his eyes from the sun. The hats brim cast his face in shadows, but Rafe didn't need to see Jesse's face to know the look being thrown at him would singe the hide off a cows ass.

Watching him march to the wagon, Rafe took off his own hat, ran his fingers through his hair and looked up at sky. "What the hell am I supposed to do now?"

Sighing, he placed his hat back on his head and started after Jesse. When he reached the wagon, he propped his foot on the wheel. "So, what are you going to do?"

Jesse snorted a laugh. "What do you think I'm going to do?"

"I don't know. That's why I asked."

"I'm going to town to pick up my wife. I done told you that."

Rafe looked toward the sky again hoping some divine answer would slap him across the face and exhaled a long breath when none came. He looked back at Jesse, the fire in his brother's eyes still shining, and he felt his temper rise again. "You can't keep her, Jesse. I won't allow it."

"You don't have no say so in it, *Big Brother*." Jesse grabbed the reins, throwing them over the front of the wagon and turned, giving Rafe his full attention. "I'm going into town and there isn't anything you can do about it."

"I can blister your hide."

"I'd like to see you try."

Rafe straightened, towering over his brother. "Don't test me, Jesse. I have enough work to do to last me clean through the winter and I don't have but a month to get it all done. I don't have time for this foolishness."

"Me getting married ain't foolish. Every man does it at some point. Hell, even you did! I'm just going to do it earlier than most."

Memories of Katie flooded Rafe's mind so quickly they almost staggered him. He pushed her away like he always did and the anger those memories brought hardened his heart just a little bit more.

Bringing Katie up seemed to accomplish what Jesse hoped it would. The boy had a smug look on his face, and the urge to strangle him until his eyes popped out of their sockets was tempting. The little fool never listened. Why did he think today would be any different, especially with this?

The kid had no idea what he was getting himself into. The woman who came to be married would take one look at Jesse and laugh. Then what? He'll come back home ornery as a bull, he thought. Just like any other day. It would serve him right to be handed his ass by some high-strung woman. Maybe she could put the kid in his place. He sure as hell couldn't.

Rafe repositioned his hat and stared his brother in the eye. There was no talking him out of this, he could see that now. He rarely could when Jesse set his mind to something. Their fights were beginning to be legendary the boys temper was so out of control, so why not let him have his way for once and let him see, first hand, what it takes to be a man?

"You know what, Jesse? You're right. I think it is time you grew up. Have a little more responsibility than I've allowed. I'll head on in with you to pick up your bride if you don't mind."

Jesse looked confused for a moment before he nodded and climbed up into the wagon. He waited for Rafe to join him before taking the reins and handing them over. Rafe held back a smile. For someone who was old enough to take a wife, you would think he could handle a wagon, and a older than dirt mule, with confidence. Just goes to show, the kid had a lot to learn yet and his brother's wife was going to give him a lesson he'd never forget.

◡

They were laughing at her. Grace Kingston's face heated, embarrassment burning her throat and landing on her face as every person in the room guffawed and belly-laughed while staring at her.

Her nervousness about making the journey across the country to marry a man sight-unseen grew ten-fold as Ellie, the stagecoach station owner, and the dozen or so men scattered around the room continued to stare after telling them the name of her intended groom.

What was wrong with the man she'd promised to marry that had an entire room full of people laughing?

She'd had a bad feeling the moment the stagecoach stopped and she was helped out to stand on the wooden sidewalk, getting her first good look at the town of Willow Creek. It resembled nothing of Boston and she knew Jesse Samuels, the man she'd agreed to marry, had lied. His descriptive letter had painted a picture in her mind that was filled with wild flowers, fields green with grass and clean mountain air, and a town teaming with life.

How disappointing to realize Willow Creek looked like every other dusty town she'd traveled through to get here.

She'd taken in the dirt road, its deep tracks carved from wagons and horse hooves. Dust seemed to cling to everything in sight and her clothing was covered in a light layer of it in a matter of minutes.

The buildings on the one and only street were lined in uneven rows, the wooden walkways unlevel and tilting toward the rutted road in most places. New construction at the end of town told her the small community was growing but it wouldn't be fast enough for her. She was used to the finer things in life. Why did she think a small pioneer town in the middle of nowhere would be anything like the city she loved, and left, to find an adventure?

Her journey so far hadn't been at all as she'd imagined. The money she'd saved to make the trip was all but gone due high priced meals and lodging along the way. The lack of proper hygiene was beginning to make its presence known as her traveling dress was stained and was starting to smell. Of course, most of the stench in the air came from the town's livery stable that sat beside the stagecoach station. The scent of manure and straw filled the air and pulling a perfumed handkerchief from the sleeve of her dress and holding it to her nose, did little to ward off the stench.

The entire situation was deplorable but she had little choice but to see her rash decision through. Which brought her back to Ellie and the men scattered around the room who still snickered at her as if she were the punch line of some joke no one bothered to tell her.

Ellie was heavy set, her graying hair pulled into a tight bun at the back of her head. She had a kind face, wrinkled from laughter and age, and Grace remembered her manners and excused herself without spouting off a biting remark at the woman's behavior. She turned on her heel and made her way back to the wooden sidewalk outside.

Grace tried her best to look calm but she was failing. Her stomach was in knots as every horrible possibility her friends had told her about screamed through her head in quick succession.

The thought of Jesse Samuels misrepresenting himself was now a reality. The reaction Ellie and the men inside the station had, had to mean something. Was her bridegroom a scoundrel instead of a rancher as he'd said? Was he lacking in some way that caused the prospect of marrying him to be so amusing to the townspeople? Was he was a drunkard or worse? A man so ugly the thoughts of giving her body to him would turn her stomach despite his fortune?

Maybe this wasn't a good idea. She knew the possibility of marrying a man who wasn't at all pleasing to the eye was possible but at the time, she felt she had little choice. It was either marry sight-unseen or marry the man she suspected of stealing her father's fortune. A chill raced up her spine at the thought. She'd marry the lowest man in all of Montana before giving that foul beast the satisfaction of having her and her father's money.

She could have changed her mind a number of times during her journey but she hadn't. She'd sold every possession she owned to pay off her father's debts and have enough to travel across the country. Now, she had no choice but to stay. She didn't have the money for a return trip home, and besides, what waited for her there left her feeling desperate.

But would her new bridegroom be just as unwelcome a sight as her old life in Boston?

She walked over to her things, grabbing her skirts before sitting down on top of her trunk, and propped her chin on her hand before sighing. She stared out across the dusty road, watched the townsfolk go about their business and prayed she hadn't made the biggest mistake of her life.

Long minutes of waiting turned into an hour. Grace tapped a heel on the wooden sidewalk and huffed out another breath. A cool breeze sent wisps of dust flurrying across the sidewalk as another wagon rolled over the rutted road. She straightened her back and peered at the driver. He lifted his hat in greeting but kept going just as every other man who passed by did.

She was about to give up hope when she spotted a smaller wagon ambling into town that seemed to be heading in her direction. A man and young boy were both looking at her as they neared the stagecoach station, and she lifted a hand to shield her face from the sun to see them. Surely this wasn't her bridegroom. The wagon was no more than a broken down wooden box with wheels.

When they stopped in front of the station, the man sat staring at her for long minutes before looking to the boy who was doing the same. Neither seemed inclined to move. She stood, stretching the kinks out of her back, and said, "Hello."

The man mumbled something to the boy before he shook his head and jumped to the ground. When he approached her, Grace felt her pulse jump and her lungs seized until she found it hard to breathe.

He was handsome and tall, with dark hair that fell to his shoulders in waves. The brown hat on his head left much of his face in shadow but she could see his eyes were green, in a shade so pale she was mesmerized just looking at them. A light dusting of whiskers was growing in on his chin.

When he stopped in front of her, Grace hoped this was the man she'd been waiting on. He fit the physical description she'd received from Jesse in the letter he sent with his request, and he was more handsome than she'd hoped he would be.

"You Grace?" he asked, repositioning his hat.

Grace nodded her head, her heart thumping in her chest. It *was* him. This was the man she was to marry. The joy she felt was overwhelming. She smiled when she realized the prospect of being stuck in this tiny town didn't seem like such a burden now. Jesse Samuels was everything she'd hoped to find. A man who was strong, handsome… and who had all his teeth. He wasn't fat nor ugly. He didn't have the look of a drunk and his eyes didn't hold that predatory glint she's seen in so many of the men she'd known in her life. He didn't look like a wealthy rancher but she supposed he wouldn't if he worked his land instead of just hiring others to do it for him.

When he did nothing more than stare at her in return, she looked away. The boy had climbed down from the wagon and was staring at her. His face was bright red, as was his hair, and Grace gave him a smile. His blush deepened before he looked away.

She managed to snap out of her stupor and returned her gaze to the man in front of her. "I was beginning to think you weren't coming."

"It's a long trip into town and that old mule can only go so fast." His gaze moved from her face to her breasts to her hips before coming back up. Grace would have been offended if it hadn't caused such a delicious tingle to run laps up and down her spine. She averted her gaze, watching the boy as he kicked at the sidewalk with the toe of his boot. He was young, long legged, and thin. He'd yet to put on any muscle she could see. He favored her new bridegroom in facial features but that was about it. Their coloring was completely different.

She smiled again, pleased her trip hadn't turned out to be a total mistake and settled her gaze back on those soft green eyes of the man standing before her. "Will we marry now or at some later date? Is there a preacher in town?"

He grinned at her before turning to the boy. "You want to go hunt down that preacher?"

Ellie chose that moment to stick her head out the door of the stagecoach station. She gave a chuckle in Grace's direction before saying, "The preacher ain't here." Nearly everyone in the stage-coach station was hovering in the doorway of the building. Ellie was smiling, amusement flashing in her eyes. "He left yesterday morning."

"Are you sure?" the youth by the wagon asked.

Ellie laughed before nodding her head. "Afraid so." She glanced at them all before looking toward Grace's bridegroom. "Afternoon, Rafe. I hear there's to be a wedding."

"Seems so."

Grace turned. She stared up at her bridegroom, the man she knew just spoke, but he didn't answer to the name Jesse. "You prefer to be called Rafe?" she asked.

He nodded. "Yep. It's the name my Ma gave me. Everyone uses it."

The snickers started again. Grace took a step to the side so she could see everyone at once and her fatigue started to take its toll. She was getting irritated as well and her confusion was growing. "All right. I'll call you Rafe as well." She smiled at him before asking, "How long will we have to wait to be wed?"

"A while I suppose. The Preacher doesn't get around to these parts but every few months." Rafe repositioned his hat again, glancing over his shoulder to the boy. "But don't worry. Jesse will do right by you. He sent for a bride and he's determined to have one."

Now Grace *was* confused. She looked at Rafe, then Ellie and the men standing in the station, before turning to look at the wagon. The redhead boy was still standing there blushing and Grace felt as if she was being pulled in endless circles. Ellie chuckled one last time before ushering the men back into the building and leaving her alone with Rafe and the boy. "It's been an extremely long day," she said. "I'm afraid I'm a bit confused."

"About what?"

"Well, everything." Grace sighed. "Are you Jesse Samuels?"

"No. I'm Rafe Samuels. Jesse's brother."

Grace's eyes widened. "Oh! Well, that explains my confusion."

She laughed, trying to mask her disappointment. "I thought you were my bridegroom."

Rafe smiled, those fine white teeth of his gleaming. His gaze traveled the length of her again, stopping to linger on her breasts for long moments before meeting her eyes. "I'm sorry to say I'm not. There's your groom." He turned and pointed toward the wagon.

The redheaded boy was still there, looking at anything but her. It took Grace only moments for Rafe's words to sink in. Jesse Samuels *was* there. He just wasn't who she thought he was. "That's Jesse?"

"Yep."

Looking up at Rafe, Grace could see amusement dancing in his eyes. He knew she'd mistaken him for Jesse and he was enjoying her stupidity. And stupid is how she felt. Not only had she agreed to marry sight-unseen, but she'd somehow promised herself to a child. A boy who was too embarrassed to even look her in the eye.

End of excerpt....

☗

Find purchase links for this book on my website at:
www.lilygraison.com/HisBrothersWife

WANT MORE?

For information about upcoming books in the Willow Creek, Silver Falls or Prison Moon Series, and any other books by Lily Graison, subscribe to her Newsletter or find her around the web at the following locations.

Website: http://lilygraison.com/
Newsletter: http://bit.ly/LilyNewsletter
Twitter: https://twitter.com/#!/LilyGraison
FaceBook: http://www.facebook.com/authorLilyGraison
Reader Group: http://bit.ly/LilyGraisonReaderGroup
Email: lily@lilygraison.com
Instagram: https://www.instagram.com/authorlilygraison/

Subscribe to email notifications of new releases here:
Newsletter: http://bit.ly/LilyNewsletter

Also by Lily Graison

HISTORICAL WESTERN ROMANCE

WILLOW CREEK SERIES

The Lawman (Willow Creek #1)

The Outlaw (Willow Creek #2)

The Gambler (Willow Creek #3)

The Rancher (Willow Creek #4)

His Brother's Wife (Willow Creek #5)

A Willow Creek Christmas (Willow Creek #6)

Wild Horses (Willow Creek #7)

Lullaby (A Willow Creek Short Story)

Nightingale (Willow Creek #8)

Heartstrings (A Willow Creek Short Story)

SILVER FALLS SERIES

A Soft Kiss in Winter (Silver Falls #1)

SCIENCE FICTION ROMANCE

Dragon Fire (Prison Moon Series)

Warlord's Mate (coming soon)

CONTEMPORARY ROMANCE

Wicked: Leather and Lace (Wicked Series #2)

Wicked: Jade Butterfly (Wicked Series #3)

Wicked: Sweet Temptation (Wicked Series #4)

Wicked: The Complete Series (Books #1 - 4)

PARANORMAL ROMANCE

The Calling (Night Breeds Duet #1)

The Gathering (Night Breeds Duet #2)

MULTI-AUTHOR PROJECTS

Anna: Bride of Alabama

(American Mail-Order Brides Series Book 22)

Julia (Angel Creek Christmas Brides Book 2)

STAND ALONE ROMANCE STORIES

Blame It On The Mistletoe (contemporary)

That First Christmas (contemporary)

ABOUT THE AUTHOR

Lily Graison is a USA TODAY bestselling author of historical western romances who has been known to dabble in sci-fi, contemporary and paranormals when the mood strikes. The author of over twenty books, her stories all lean heavily toward the spicy side with strong female characters and heroes who tend to always get their way. She writes full time and lives in Hickory, NC with her husband and a house full of Yorkies.

Website: http://lilygraison.com/
Or Email Lily at: lily@lilygraison.com